GOTTA WEAR ECLIPSE GLASSES

Third Flatiron Anthologies
Volume 9, Book 28, Summer 2020

Edited by Juliana Rew
Cover Art by Keely Rew

Gotta Wear Eclipse Glasses
Third Flatiron Anthologies
Volume 9, Summer 2020

Published by Third Flatiron Publishing
Juliana Rew, Editor and Publisher

Copyright 2020 Third Flatiron Publishing
ISBN #978-1-7339207-7-3

Discover other titles by Third Flatiron:

License Notes

Contents

*****~~~~~*****

Editor's Note

We are all feeling shut in during the C-19 coronavirus pandemic, so Third Flatiron wants to reach out to our many friends and readers, to give back a little of the support we've received over the years. We will be offering the ebook of *Gotta Wear Eclipse Glasses* free during this period to help anyone whose discretionary reading funds might be tight.

The theme of this science fiction and fantasy anthology is "the future we'd all like to see." This doesn't mean it all has to be rainbows and balloons, but some optimism and brightness don't hurt a bit. Besides returning authors from previous anthologies, we are pleased to feature three stories by Colorado authors, as well as first publications by new writers.

Weird is wonderful: We lead off with Robert Bagnall's "The Thirteenth Floor," a fascinating trip to an invisible world that's sitting right in front of us. (Probably.)

A little help from our friends: Artificially intelligent creatures designed to serve humanity begin to realize that social distancing is not their thing, as in Alexandra Seidel's "We Make Life Beautiful Again." Patrick Hurley's police constable becomes a crime-solving

7

whiz when augmented by his AI partner in "The Centaur Detective and the Vanishing Man."

Pokémon Ultra: Several of our contributors this time delved into future cyberpunk. Some of their characters use augmented reality and implants to play games, as in Koji A. Dae's "SoulShine," while others just use VR to blot out a crumbling world, as in David Cleden's "All Fuzzed Out and Fractal." Either way, it may be costly to your soul.

Anywhere but here: To some, a best possible future might be Heaven on Earth, but others look to quantum mechanics for something even better, as in Eneasz Brodski's "Give Me My Wings."

Taste l'Arc en Ciel: A boy's family helps reintroduce giraffes to their native African home in Gustavo Bondoni's "Such Sweet Sorrow." (See? Rainbows and balloons.)

To see a loved one again: A grieving mother and daughter (and the dog and the goldfish) find that their new life is "Just Like Living with Dad," as told by Jenny Blackford.

Wouldn't it be nice to have a "Catcher in the Sky" to remove carbon from the atmosphere, asks Paul A. Freeman. And Liam Hogan's alien visitors treat a young vlogger to a tour of their "Lighter Than Air" cities.

The best rock concert ever, and you're there: After the apocalypse, join the Battle of the Bands in Angelique Fawns' "The New Mutants."

A fresh start: A young girl survives a ski accident, and has her clone to thank for it in Emily Martha Sorensen's "Tabula Rasa."

Hey, Aquaman: Earth's oceans shelter humanity from the ravages on land in Christopher Muscato's underwater adventure, "Living As You, Our City a Garden."

To the Stars and Beyond: When the first of the pioneers aboard a colony ship die, a young descendant

8

learns the meaning of "Ashes to Ashes," in Chloie Piveral's touching story.

For the good of all: Though not everyone agrees that geoengineering the climate is a good idea, Mike Adamson's straight-shooting space warrior does her level best to ensure the return of "The First Day of Winter." And though most of future humanity has learned the value of peace, as in Neil James Hudson's "War's End," we might want to hold a little in reserve, just in case…

. . .

Grins & Gurgles: To close the anthology, we proffer a bit of lightness in our flash humor section.

Wordplay: "Lexophile" describes those that have a love for words, such as "you can tune a piano, but you can't tuna fish," and "To write with a broken pencil is pointless." Mariev, Erie Matriarch, cracks us up expertly with "For Mom: Standup Cosmic Comedy."

A bit of common sense wins out in Matt Tighe's "The Plumber."

Stiff upper lip: Ville Nummenpää's "Interview with a Zombie" starts out well, until everything falls apart.

To see ourselves as others see us: A colonist has a little "Night Chat" with some tiny Martians in this fun story by John Kiste.

Enjoy! Thanks for reading, and stay safe,

Juliana Rew, Editor
May 2020

*****~~~~*****

Living As You, Our City a Garden

by Christopher Muscato

Soshi tried not to inhale, desperately clenching his jaw and pursing his lips as his cheeks turned red. His dark hair danced, wild in the current. Floating there, surrounded by a wild sea, Soshi fought and fought. And then he could fight no longer.

With a great gasp, his lips burst open and saltwater poured into his lungs.

"I win!" cheered Mina, splashing around victoriously. Bent over, grasping his knees and panting, Soshi glared at his younger sister.

"You cheated," he asserted, although he knew he lacked any evidence to support the dubious accusation.

"Mina! Soshi! Breakfast!"

With a flurry of webbed hands, Soshi and Mina raced through their home, pushing at each other and twirling through the water. Soshi's feet brushed against the sea grass that was their floor as he accepted the spherical ceramic bowl filled with seaweed-wrapped fish from his mother. The meal was inhaled nearly as quickly as it was served.

"Soshi! Chew!" chided his mother, shaking her head as she helped Mina with her chopsticks. Soshi started coughing on a bit of seaweed caught in his throat, and his mother groaned, releasing an exasperated sigh. "Please tell me you at least finished packing."

"Almosht," Soshi replied through stuffed cheeks, air bubbles punctuating his words. Mina giggled gleefully at the sight.

"Shimizu Soshi you go and finish packing right away! We have to leave for the city in less than an hour!"

"Mom, is it true that all people used to live on the land and not the sea?" Mina asked suddenly, poking at a passing hermit crab with her chopsticks.

"Yes, dear. Now eat. Leave the crab alone."

"Told ya," whispered Soshi.

"Soshi! Go pack!"

. . .

"Soshi-chan, good to see you!"

"Hello Gamizu-san," Soshi bowed politely as he bobbed in the water, the long fabric of his finest dress robes swirling around him.

"Soshi."

"Yui-senpai," Soshi bowed again to the teenage girl, fighting the urge to turn the bow into a somersault. Yui smiled warmly.

"Yui!" Mina screamed, paddling frantically towards the teenager and wrapping around her. Yui laughed.

"Hi, Mina! Are you excited to go to the city?"

Mina nodded somberly. She had waited a long time for this. Soshi was pretty eager too, not that he would show it. It wasn't every day they got to go to the city.

The two families loaded their belongings into the ray-shaped rig, securing supplies and tying down the ropes. The propellers sputtered to life, and the rig skirted agilely along the seafloor, kicking up diaphanous clouds of glistening sand in its wake.

"Yui, what makes the rig go?" Mina asked.

"You see these vents? The water moves through them and rotates turbines in the engine. That motion makes energy and powers the rig," Yui explained as Mina stared, mouth agape. Soshi brushed his hair out of his eyes and leaned against the side of the winged rig, fidgeting in his harness, and watched their home shrink into the distance until it was indistinguishable from the rocks and reef surrounding it. Along the seafloor, beams of sunlight danced over the sand in hypnotic ribbons. A flicker of a shadow passed overhead, and Soshi looked up, hoping it might be a whale. It was a large school of fish, but he did think he saw a turtle passing through it.

"Did you hear that the Sato baby came early?" Soshi heard his mother inform Mr. Gamizu from the front of the rattling rig.

"No! Is he okay?"

"Baby and momma are fine, thank goodness, but his gills weren't strong enough yet, so he's in an oxygen chamber until he's ready to breath seawater."

The conversations continued in much their usual ways, updates on reef gossip, elections for the Kokkai, prices of seaweed, marine conditions. For krill-farming families such as theirs, such topics were never exhaustible. Mina asked Yui why humanity went underwater. Yui attempted to explain how people had almost destroyed the entire world, but were able to figure out how to neutralize the acidity within the ocean long before they could fix the problems with the air and the land. They would have to move underwater to survive, and genetic splicing made it possible, altering human evolution and saving the species from extinction on the fire-ravished and nutrient-depleted land. The few tribes that stayed above continued to ravage the environment, relentless and unwavering.

"Just because some humans still live on land, it doesn't make them monsters," Soshi's mother interjected from the front of the rig. "We still interact with them.

13

They sell us our dried spices. They just haven't learned to be part of their ecosystems."

"And they never will," Mr. Gamizu grumbled. "How much effort do we put into negating the effects of their actions on our reefs? Every year, it never ends!"

"But they have made progress in reducing their seagoing pollution," Soshi's mother reminded them. "That's an important step towards coexistence."

Mr. Gamizu snorted indignantly.

"As long as they stay on land and we stay in the water, we'll all get along fine."

Soshi had heard ghost stories from friends about the land-dwellers, savages who would see their dry world burned to ash before giving up their ravenous ways. But, his mother didn't seem in the mood to entertain such tales, and so Soshi waited patiently through the lessons and the gossip, webbed fingers tapping rhythmically on the side of the rig, counting passing fish, scanning the cerulean depths, until finally—

"There it is!" Soshi shouted so loudly and so suddenly that everyone, including Mr. Gamizu at the helm of the rig, jumped. Soshi's admonishment by his mother would be short-lived, however, because after all, he was right. There it was.

The great city's appearance was heralded by splashes of light, crystalizing from the blue and disappearing just as effortlessly, whirling throughout the seascape and casting the rig in a kaleidoscope of reflected light and playful shadow. The great schools of fish scattered as the rig passed, then merged back together once it was gone, resuming their dance.

Soshi's eyes were so wide he thought they might pop from his head and float up to the surface, a fate his mother promised every time he made this expression. Rigs competed with each other for positioning as lanes merged, solitary fish darting between them, the occasional ray gliding overhead. Denizens of the city swam from shop to

14

shop, touting their wares, sharing their gossip, conducting their business on the many levels of the aqueous cityscape. Everywhere he looked, the city was alive.

Soshi's neck began to ache as he strained to see the tops of the massive structures surrounding him. Offices, restaurants, apartments. Every building a backbone to the reef, anchored by artificial cores but built into such imposing edifices by billions of microscopic organisms. The city breathed with the colors and texture of coral. Starfish clung to the sides of banks. Eels and lobsters slunk between nooks and crannies of the shops. Soshi stared jealously at a young girl floating next to the door to her apartment, gleefully playing tug with her tentacled pet. Soshi once tried to adopt an octopus that had wandered through their krill farm, but his mom said it needed to be left to be part of the ecosystem. Plus, he wasn't ready for the responsibility.

The rig steadily traversed the canyons between reef-buildings so massive they seemed to risk breaking the surface. Wavescrapers, Soshi's mother called these towers. Yui pointed out hatcheries and various manicured habitats, from sea grass beds to kelp forests, that made this one of the most complex managed ecosystems in the Pacific. Although pretending not to care, Soshi listened to Yui out of the corners of his ears, eagerly absorbing the information and secretly admiring her depth of knowledge about such an overwhelming place. As for Mina, she had barely uttered a syllable since the city appeared, her face frozen in an expression of unyielding awe.

Finally, the rig pulled into a small alleyway, cloaked in the shadows of the adjacent wavescrapers, and docked in an open recess among a bank of horizontal niches in the side of the building. Soshi spun in the water as he stretched his legs, the other occupants of the rig following after him and floating for a few moments, pulling at their own limbs after the long ride.

"Okay Soshi, Mina, we can't build the expansion on the farm until we've consulted with an ecologist, so I need you both to be on your best behavior," Soshi's mother coached, sinking down to look her children head-on and taking their hands. Soshi and his sister eyed each other, absorbing the gravity of the upcoming meeting.

"You know, Niko-san," came Mr. Gamizu's voice, unexpectedly. He stretched an arm across his body. "What if Soshi and Mina go help Yui inspect our power station?"

Soshi felt his gills go stiff. Had he heard that right? His mother rotated slowly, stiffly, in the water, her face suddenly uneasy.

"Oh, don't worry!" Mr. Gamizu boomed, his face breaking into a wide grin. "There's no need for them to sit through this boring meeting, and Yui's been a dozen times. They'll be fine!" He turned to address Soshi directly, hands on his hips. "You'd like to see the surface, wouldn't you?"

Soshi could feel his heart pounding in his chest. He looked at his mother, hoping, pleading with his eyes. She chewed her lips for a moment, and her normally proud shoulders drooped.

"All right. Just be careful," she sighed.

. . .

"Do you know what this is, Soshi?" Yui asked as she unhinged the lid of the large metal box, removing a massive wad of orange material from inside. Soshi observed the object. Its texture was unlike anything they had in his house. It was soft, but not like sea grass, smooth like a dolphin but even more waxy. This must be a synthetic. Soshi knew that things made of artificial materials were pretty rare nowadays.

"It's called a buoy," Yui continued. "When I pull this chord, it will start to inflate with air and pull us up to the surface, so we need to tether ourselves to it and hold on tight, okay Soshi? Okay Mina?"

Living As You, Our City a Garden

Mina's head bobbed up and down, pigtails stirring up bubbles in the current. Soshi nodded as well, hoping his consciously deliberate movements didn't betray his budding nerves. For reassurance he examined the buoy personally, convincing himself that he knew what he was looking at as Yui fit Mina into her harness. Soshi peered upwards at the thick cable, shooting towards the heavens. He inspected the tether that connected the buoy to the cable, and checked the harness. All seemed to be in order.

Before long, the three youths were each situated into their harnesses, and with a confident nod, Yui pulled the chord. The orange rubber buoy started to inflate, and as it did, lifted off the sea floor, tracing the cable upwards. Mina's eyes bulged from her head as her hair whipped in her face. Yui brushed her own hair aside, abandoning her controlled demeanor and grinning exuberantly as they sped towards the surface. Soshi tried to relax his muscles and, as he did, found he was able to enjoy the ride.

It would only take them about ten minutes to reach the surface. Sure they could swim, but this took much less effort. Soshi shrugged his shoulders, rolled his neck, and squirmed, his body adjusting to the gradual decompression. He tried to shake it off and chanced a few glimpses around. From here at the outskirts of city, he could see the rooftops of the structures of the reef, the glistening of the throngs of fish and people still dancing in the sunbeams. New construction zones, where trash that couldn't be decomposed was recycled into setting the foundations for new reef, dotted the edges of the cityscape. To his sides, Soshi saw only a forest of barnacle-covered wires, swaying pillars of thin black lines offset by sparkling beams of sunlight that penetrated the murky depths. Soshi looked up, and saw glistening patches of sky and sun, splashed together like a cloud of yellow and white and blue clay that swirled in the current.

Quite unexpectedly, Yui seized his and Mina's hands and squeezed tight. With a thunderous splashing and a blast of cool, the buoy punctured the waves.

"Breathe, Soshi, Mina. Look at me; just breathe. Let your lungs adjust."

Soshi's white fingers clutched his heaving chest, his vision blurry, his ears ringing. Yui's voice remained steady, anchoring him, and steadily the world around him came into focus. His breathing slowed, and he held his hand out. It was heavy, unused to supporting its own weight, chilled by its first exposure to dry air and yet simultaneously warmed by such direct contact with unfiltered sunlight. Soshi took in few more slow breaths, and looked first to his sister and then Yui, grinning widely.

Yui permitted Soshi and Mina several minutes to observe the blue sky and bright sun, the waves splashing against their faces, cheers wafting through the air, but she soon reminded them that they couldn't be exposed to surface conditions for too long and they still had a chore to do.

The surface was dotted with reflective black rectangles and bobbing spheres, all connected to the web of power cables through which they had just risen. Yui identified these floating objects as panels and turbines that collected energy from the sunlight and the motion of the waves and converted these to usable power. Every family who lived in the jurisdiction of the city was responsible for maintaining a section of the grid, and in that way everybody shared in the responsibility and everyone shared in the rewards.

Yui guided Soshi and Mina to her family's turbines, and then to theirs, showing them how to run diagnostics on the machines, how to download the data, how to clean them. They were nearly done when Soshi, splashing some water in his dry face, thought he heard a noise. He cocked his head.

18

"What is that?"

Yui looked up from what she was doing, and froze.

"Soshi, Mina, dive. Now."

"Wh-what?"

"I said now! There's no time to let the buoy deflate. Dive, now!" And with that she plunged into the sea, pulling them with her.

Furiously, the three swam, Yui pulling the younger two as they struggled to keep up. Then, all at once she stopped, clutching them to her and clinging to the cable for whatever minuscule protection it might afford. With eyes wide, Soshi scanned their surroundings. The rumbling noise he had heard earlier grew louder, and he looked up to see a monstrous shadow pass overhead, shaking the waves in its violent wake as it disappeared into the distance.

"What is it?" Mina whispered in her brother's ear, her voice quivering with such terror that she could barely get the syllables out.

"I think it's a boat, Mina. How land-dwellers move on the water." Soshi looked to Yui for confirmation, but Yui was not listening. Nor was she looking up where the boat had passed. Instead, face drained entirely of color, she was staring at the space directly beneath them. Soshi gulped and forced himself to turn his head down, then felt his courage dissolve. Already below them, there were three figures descending slowly down the cables, crisp lines of tiny bubbles flowing from dark masks obscuring their faces. The land-dwellers were somehow under the sea.

"Soshi. . . " With Mina's barely audible whisper, Soshi felt a tug on his shoulder, and he followed his sister's gaze outwards. More figures were emerging from the shadows in every direction, streams of bubbles steadily forming the bars of an effervescent cage. The swimming land-dwellers had surrounded them.

Gotta Wear Eclipse Glasses

"What do we do?" Soshi whispered to Yui, who had regained her composure and whose eyes now burned with determination and whose forehead wrinkled with focus.

"I don't think they see us yet, so we'll pull ourselves down the cable to the sea floor. I'll go first, Mina you stay behind me, and Soshi you take the rear," Yui said finally, steadily. "We'll go slow. Hopefully we can at least get closer to the city."

"What if they see us?" asked Soshi, hands trembling. Yui thought it over.

"Then take Mina and swim towards the city as fast as you can. Don't stop and don't look back," she answered resolutely. She looked him directly in the eyes. "It will be okay. I'm counting on you to watch our backs and to keep your sister safe, okay? I trust you."

The words pierced Soshi, and he felt his chest swell. He clenched his fists to stop his fingers from shaking, and he nodded firmly.

The trio oriented themselves along the cable, Yui, Mina, Soshi, and began the painfully slow descent into the depths. Soshi looked continuously around, remaining faithful to his anointed duties as rear sentinel. So far, the swimming land-dwellers had not seemed to notice them. Instead, the strangers were so totally engaged in inspecting the cables and wires of the power stations that Soshi wondered if even the monstrous awakening of an ancient kaiju from the depths would catch their attention.

There was a comfort to that thought as the three tried to remain invisible to the intruders, although Soshi could not figure out why these marauders were so thoroughly distracted by something so mundane. The land-dwellers poked and prodded at the cables, measuring them and holding up strange instruments, but no part of this process seemed invasive or destructive. It was curious. Soshi had heard stories about land-dwellers from friends, and none of these tales inspired much confidence

20

in those who lived above the water. It was said that they consumed everything in their paths, sometimes including even each other. Hitomu claimed that they were too savage to learn how to breathe underwater. Kousuke insisted that his uncle was nearly speared by land-dwellers while trading with them at the surface. He even bore the scar on his forearm to prove it.

Soshi gulped, water flushing through his gills, and tried not to think about these stories. He had a job to do, watching their backs, and he had to be brave. He had to.

For what seemed an eternity even more boundless than the sea itself, the three methodically worked their way down the endless cable, hand over webbed hand, until finally something solid began to materialize from the blue. It was the sea floor. They were almost there. Soshi paused and hastily surveyed the scene. Most of the land-dwellers appeared to have remained near the surface, occupied with whatever they were doing to the cables and solar panels and turbines. Only a few intrepid intruders had actually followed the cables to the bottom, taking rests along the way, and were now drifting around the sea grass, pointing at the wires of the power grid.

Circumventing these land-dwellers would not be easy. Soshi dedicated his attention to developing a strategy, although few of his initial ideas seemed highly practical barring the sudden discovery that he could summon a giant squid with his mind. Maybe it was at least worth trying.

Soshi was engaged in this line of thought when he happened to glance up, and felt his blood run cold. One of the land-dwellers, still floating a distance away, was staring directly at them.

The murky figure slowly lifted an arm, never taking its masked face off of Soshi, blindly flapping a hand around behind it until finally making contact with a neighboring land-dweller. That figure waved off the attack and looked up, raising its shielded head and then freezing

21

upon observing the three young sea-dwellers clinging to the cable several meters away.

"Yui," Soshi whispered. It took her only a second to realize what was causing his voice to quiver.

"You remember what we talked about, Soshi? As fast as you can. Don't look back." And with that she launched from the cable, jetting directly towards the submerged interlopers. Soshi seized his sister's hand, catching a final glimpse of the land-dwellers dropping their equipment at Yui's advance and spinning out of control as they waved their arms and legs about like newborn seals. Soshi pushed against the cable, pulling Mina with him, but had barely begun to paddle when several more figures appeared in front of them.

Soshi backpedaled, kicking up a cloud of sand and bubbles, and changed direction. That way too was blocked by land-dwellers, all waving their arms and web-less hands furiously over their heads. Was this some form of land-dweller war dance? Soshi pulled his sister closer, trying to control his panicked breathing.

"It will be okay Mina. I've got you. It will be okay."

The masked swimmers, bouncing along the sea floor, were slowly converging. Soshi spun around and around, looking for the best path through which to escape. The land-dwellers looked back and forth at each other, hesitating as they approached, their movements cautious and unsure. Finally, one of them stepped out from the others, palms extended outwards. Soshi gripped his sister tighter, unsure how to interpret the gesture.

The masked figure, moving at a pace Soshi thought would even drive a sea slug mad, produced from its belt a small cylinder, bending low and placing it on the sandy sea floor, keeping one palm extended throughout the entire ritual. The figure straightened up, stepped back, looked directly at Soshi, and did something he never expected: it bowed.

With that, the entire ring of land-dwellers started taking small and deliberate steps backwards, floating off the ground and swimming off, regrouping in a small cluster a respectful distance away.

Mina looked up at Soshi, still tightly wrapped in his protective grip. He spun around, waiting for the trap to spring, but nothing came. The cylinder glistened tauntingly among the short patches of swaying sea grass. Soshi spun around again. Still nothing. Curiosity tugged at his mind. The land-dwellers remained huddled in the distance, barely moving. Slowly, Soshi reached out with a cautious but steady hand. In an explosion of sand, he snatched the cylinder from the ground and sped off towards the city, dragging Mina along with him.

. . .

"Could it be a trap?" Soshi could hear Mr. Gamizu's voice from the other room. After their mad dash from the power stations, Soshi and Mina had sought refuge in the first grotto they encountered, disturbing a particularly grumpy grouper, and were finally found by Yui as they floated in the dark, panting. Soshi showed her the strange cylinder and she had started to inspect it, suddenly dropping the object as it shook to life and the hologram materialized, the glowing light filling the cave and the voice echoing off the walls.

"If they really do want to learn from us," Soshi's mother was now raising her voice, "we can't let ghost stories cloud our judgment."

Soshi pulled the blanket tighter around his sister, holding her close as they waited outside the mayor's office in the city hall, the room comfortably padded with sea sponges. Yui looked at him, and smiled.

"You did good, Soshi," she said, tussling his hair. Soshi felt his cheeks start to burn and he shrugged modestly.

"And your children said they're still there, outside the reef?" the mayor asked. "Could be a trap."

23

"Could be the start of something much bigger, Shichou-san. Something better."

Soshi ran the message through his mind. He didn't fully understand it, but the messenger spoke of living in a garden. Soshi liked that.

About the Author

Christopher Muscato is an adjunct instructor in Greeley, Colorado, and the 2017 High Plains Library District's Writer-in-Residence, and yes, he's hiked the Flatirons several times! He has short stories recently published in the January edition of *The Gateway Review* and an anthology called *The Shitlist*, as well as a flash fiction suite recently judged as a finalist and popular vote runner-up in a contest by Defenestrationism.net.

*****~~~~~*****

The Thirteenth Floor

by Robert Bagnall

MONDAY

"Jimmy, I'm turning forty. Do you know what that means?"

"Big party?"

"Jimmy, I found a grey hair," Alison persisted.

"Dye it."

"There's only so much you can dye."

A moment's awkward silence as a braying suit at the bar put in an order for champagne. Perhaps his day had been spent dotting the i's and crossing the t's on a deal made over kitesurfing at the weekend. Nobody says you can't sign off and celebrate on a Monday.

"What are you saying? You've made enough to retire to the Caribbean? You gonna spend your mornings sanding the upturned hull of a boat on a beach and your evenings drinking cocktails? You'll look like a rom-com movie poster."

It'll happen to you, too, Alison thought. She had always been one step ahead. Unsurprising, since she had been assigned to mentor Jimmy when he walked into the offices of Reingold's ten years earlier, fresher faced than he was now. And, following hard on the heels of that

25

thought, if Jimmy was fresh faced then, how must she look. . .

"What I'm saying is that there's only so many days you can throw yourself into the fire. I used to get in that lift in the morning mentally fist-punching. Now, I'm hesitating to pick up the phone."

"So, what are you going to do?"

"I'm putting together a deal. Walkers have a book of loans that they want rid of. With a little repackaging, it can be made to look attractive to a pension company I have an in with."

Jimmy looked blank. He still didn't know what it felt like to have the fear in this business. "You're back deal-making. Fist pumps at dawn."

"The deal may include me."

"Walkers?"

"No, the pension company."

"Pensions. Is that really where you want to go? Slow lane of the rat race?"

Alison laughed as Jimmy shared out the rest of the bottle, thinking, *please don't let him talk me into another. It's Monday.*

"Slow lane? Way I'm feeling, let me pull over and stop. Smell the flowers."

TUESDAY

One more bottle, Jimmy had said. Christ, on a Monday. Bleary, Alison stepped in the elevator and stabbed at the buttons. She'd aimed for ten but caught thirteen immediately below.

It lit briefly and then went out.

Alone, her brain still processing sauvignon blanc, she was fascinated. Ten lit and stayed lit, she found, as the lift lurched upwards. But not thirteen. She kept pressing. What was that definition of madness? Doing the same thing over and over, always expecting a different outcome.

26

Eleven, twelve, and every floor from fourteen upwards lit like a full moon. Even the executive suite on twenty-two. But not thirteen.

And, as she approached her own trading floor, she found she could light up all the single-digit numbers. A full house highlighting a single dull island.

Getting out, a knot of people waited by the doors. It looked like a senior partner and prospective recruits. No, she thought, body language too confident: clients.

She caught a confused, irritated bleat as they entered the elevator. "I know. Some joker," she called back, covering.

Alison went through her callback list powered by strong coffee, deluding herself that the faster she worked the faster the clock would turn. It was mid-morning before she caught Jimmy at the watercooler.

"What's on thirteen?"

"What's on thirteen what?" He thought it was a joke.

"The thirteenth floor."

"Isn't that personnel, legal, compliance, audit? You know, the overheads?"

"They're on fifteen."

"All of them?"

"How many do we need?"

. . .

On her way home Alison paused and turned to look at the building she worked in. A flood of suits and shoulder-pads, herd mentality, swept towards her, eyes tired after long hours on terminal and telephone. They moved around her, silently resentful of the impediment.

Behind the human tide stood Reingold Tower, a glass and steel beacon in a sea of glass and steel beacons. She never understood why corporate offices were kept lit at night. There was a girl from Human Resources who was constantly hectoring them to recycle, but the firm kept the bulbs burning. Go figure.

But across the structure, two-thirds up, like a pensioner's belt, was a stripe of black, where no bulbs burnt. She counted, but she knew before she started which floor it would be.

Thirteen.

She stared a moment longer, and then turned and continued on.

WEDNESDAY

"You know how you don't see what's not there? I looked through the intranet at the staff contact list. There's nobody on thirteen."

"That must have made for a fascinating lunch break," Jimmy smirked. The thirteenth floor was becoming a *not that again* topic.

"Okay, I copied and pasted it into Excel and ordered it by floor when I was on hold. Took seconds. Point being, there's nobody on thirteen."

"Maybe we're like a hotel that just goes twelve, then fourteen," Jimmy breezed.

"No, there's a floor actually there."

"That's the power of merchant banking. We can afford to ignore a real floor rather than just a number."

She gave him a hard stare.

"It's probably just sublet."

"In the middle of our floors? We own the building."

From the vantage of the watercooler, Alison scanned her colleagues, glued to screens and telephones, as if any of them could give her away at any second, a finger-point and a scream. The idea of the thirteenth floor had become fixed in her mind, blowing up to something whose name could not be spoken. *The first rule of the thirteenth floor. . .* No, wait. Wrong movie. She felt more like a character from "The Great Escape," scuffing tunnel dirt into the exercise yard via her trouser legs.

"Let's go there," Jimmy said casually. "Let's take a look."

"The lift. Remember?"

"We'll take the stairs."

Alison was suddenly a petrified animal, caught in headlights.

Jimmy shrugged. "Stairwell meeting. Brief me about your pensions deal."

"I can't," she stammered.

"No, I mean the official deal. For Reingold. Not your," and he silently mouthed *new job*. "Anyway, that's not what we'll be doing anyway, so try to get some blood back to your face."

. . .

Conspiratorial. That's how Alison felt as she walked towards the fire escape doors at the corner of the floor, one step behind Jimmy. She felt people knew what she was thinking.

A second voice in her head told her that was ridiculous and that she knew it. Her mind flitted back to a fashion magazine article on people having sex in the workplace. She never saw anything, but, if *Vogue* or *Marie Claire* were to be believed, then everybody was pairing off in the toilets all the time. Who? When? If she couldn't tell by looking, why was she convinced everybody else could read her like a book? She didn't even notice anybody look up from their terminals as she and Jimmy entered the stairwell. Almost disappointing.

Three floors up they were greeted with a firedoor, unopenable from the stairwell. Through the door's glass panel all was dark. Even cupping her hands around her face and pressing her nose close she could see nothing. She stared until, with nothing to anchor herself, she began to feel herself floating. She wondered why she had expected anything different.

"You know there's a city in Britain which they missed off the privatization legislation, you know,

29

telecoms, postal service, so forth, so it's got its own corporations and they paint the telephone boxes white, not red. I think it's called Hell."

"I think you'll find it's called Hull."

"Maybe this is like that."

Alison fixed him with a glare. "What? You mean we've just forgotten the existence of this floor? Missed it out of our plans?"

Jimmy shrugged.

"Next you'll be telling me we're the only ones who can see it."

"That was my next thought."

THURSDAY

All the previous night Alison tossed and turned.

In her dreams she was back at that firedoor, pressed up tight, staring through the glazed strip. And in her dreams, in the darkness, she could see a light. A flashing red light.

She awoke unsure what was dream and what was real. It preoccupied her. By ten that morning she realized that she'd made three vital calls about which she could remember nothing. She had to get back to the thirteenth floor. As she passed his workstation Jimmy was on a call, spinning a pen around his fingers, majorette-style, his eyes sparkling with sell sell sell. She would have to go alone.

Staring through the glazed door panel into the thirteenth floor's darkness yet again she wondered why she had ever believed in a flashing red light in the void. The dream suddenly seemed so far away and faded. Like a soap bubble bursting.

And it was at that moment that she involuntarily reeled backwards and screamed.

Momentarily, she took it to be her own face reflected back. But her own face didn't have a beard. Or small round John Lennon glasses. Or an expression of intense irritation.

As if to confirm that it was definitely not a reflection, the face on the other side of the glass remained in place, watching, taking her in. Perhaps there was a modicum of concern for her as she sprawled on the stairwell landing.

But Alison couldn't be sure, because a moment later it vanished.

FRIDAY

The two partners sat across from Alison. Against the floor-to-ceiling windows of the boardroom they were cast in partial silhouette, like wraiths. Scudding clouds reflected off the waxed and polished maple of the table. They were waiting for Alison to respond.

"That's a breach," she stuttered. "That's gotta be a breach of something."

"Could you respond to the points made in the recording we have just listened to, Miss Cornish," said Judd, all MVP thrust and metrosexual grooming.

Alison ground her teeth. She kept telling herself that she ought to be the one throwing the book at them. But when you're on the canvas because of a low blow, you're still on the canvas.

"I set that deal up. Nobody else did. Reingold will get a healthy commission because of it."

"Maybe," said Judd, "but not as much as we should or would have got had you not been sweetening the deal in order to move to Layun Assurance." He scribbled a few runic lines on his pad. Doodle or mind map? Upside down, Alison couldn't tell.

"Well?" he demanded.

She couldn't very well deny it. She had said as much, her own voice played back to her from Judd's tablet, chirpily steering the conversation towards the contractual minutiae of her new employment.

The incongruously named Marigold Bunn, a name which summoned up images of a bucolic farmer's wife or

31

red-faced charwomen, but, as Jimmy put it, was more akin to Satan's motivation coach, stiffened in her seat.

"Layun may be happy that you'll end up doing to them what you intend to do to us, but what about your next employer? People who have a reputation in the City tend to wash up somewhere downriver."

"Metaphorically," Judd added hastily with a dismissive wave.

Even against the glare of the windows Alison sensed Bunn raise a contradictory eyebrow at him.

"You can't just go around recording employees. We have rights. It's a breach. It's inadmissible."

"We're not in court, Miss Cornish," Marigold Bunn stabbed.

"But that's where we're heading."

Judd held up a hand for calm. "Oddly, it would be a breach if we *were* recording a conversation you were having with an external party."

Alison choked back a laugh. "What do you mean? Jennifer Shaw *is* external. She's at Layun Assurance."

"Jennifer Shaw is a construct. Our construct. She is not real."

Alison once dated a guy who appeared at first, second, and third glance entirely normal but, somewhere between main and dessert, suddenly asserted that the lizard people ran the planet, and he knew this because he'd seen them, seen them remove the face of God from their own phizogs and reveal their true selves. The previous moment they'd been discussing *Tess of the D'Urbervilles*. She felt the same now.

From the expressions of the two partners sat across from her, she could tell that they were deadly serious. Even Judd had stopped doodling.

"This is the thirteenth floor, isn't it?" she almost whispered.

"Perhaps I could explain."

For the first time Alison realized that there was a fourth person in the room, sitting in the darkest corner of the boardroom, perfectly still. Against the light Alison had to squint to take him in: an unusually spherical head, a wiry beard that gave way to a frizzy ponytail that had not been noticeable through the glazed porthole of the fire door. From his accent she guessed at Korean.

"Machines are now at the point where they can process natural language. Add that to their innate ability to analyze data and make decisions faster and more accurately than we ever could, and you don't need to be a machine to work out what form competitive advantage will take. Artificial intelligence will surpass human intelligence in the next two years. Regulation sets the parameters and machine learning, self-learning algorithms do the rest. Predictive analytics, recommendation engines, voice recognition and response: these are our weapons, and the thirteenth floor is our war room."

He even spoke like a machine.

"Alison," Judd said, leaning in, sounding like he was consoling the bereaved. "Do you have any idea of the power of placing deal-making in the hands of the machines? The speed of transactions, the accuracy of decisions? The escape from all those biases that the human animal is prone to?"

She found herself shaking her head in disbelief. "You've got the bleeding edge technology, and you want first mover advantage in using it to make the market. I get it. But why are you telling me all this?"

Judd continued as though Alison had never spoken. "But do you know the fundamental barrier to machine intelligence taking over Wall Street? Or the City of London? Frankfurt? Singapore?"

Unsure whether this was a rhetorical question, Alison murmured in the negative. She was feeling punch drunk, off-balance, discombobulated.

Marigold Bunn took up the running, sounding uncharacteristically placating. "Humans like dealing with humans. It's in our nature. The machine intelligence we have pioneered gives us an edge, but we won't find people to deal with if they think that we're nothing but ones and zeroes."

"I don't understand. I brokered a deal with Layun, with Jennifer Shaw. Didn't I?"

"At first. But, at some point, you both found yourself dealing with artificial intelligence, your initial contacts carried over by voice synthetization."

"But what I did is nothing. Anybody who hears the tapes. . . I fished for a new job. It's not exactly Enron."

Judd laughed softly and tapped at the tablet again. Another recording, Alison's voice, explaining why she wanted to join the pension company, how she was sick of the macho me-me-me deal, how she preferred to make a million people one dollar richer rather than one person a million dollars richer, even if that person was her. How she wanted to return some dignity to banking.

"Yeah." It was all Alison could say. She felt rather small and foolish.

"That's exactly why we want you on the inside," Judd declared, snapping his fingers, a pre-arranged signal through the glass to somebody outside. "Yes, we have first mover advantage, but we want to use it to return banking to something noble. Imagine a market with perfect knowledge, with perfect decision making. Now, imagine that market working for the little guy, the corner five-and-dime, the family-run lumber mill. Imagine a market without greed. Imagine a market that makes everybody just that little bit safer, more comfortable, more able to make dreams come true. Imagine a market that gives everybody a little, rather than one or two a lot. Imagine merchant banking. . . without merchant bankers."

Jimmy walked in, handed a folder to Marigold Bunn. "It was fun, watching you, waiting for you to be caught," he said gnomically to Alison.

Bunn withdrew a document from the folder and slid it across to Alison. It was headed *Contract*.

"Two years is all we ask," Bunn explained. "Two years for you to be a front for the machines, and then the world can reconcile itself to the fact that it was the machines making the deals all along."

"We need to put up people to be seen to be the deal-maker. To look like merchant bankers amongst the other merchant bankers, but, unlike them, we need them not to have lost their souls on the way," Judd said, and held up his doodle for her approval. "We want people like you."

It may have made sense to him but, against the light, it wasn't in the least bit clear what he was showing her.

About the Author

Robert Bagnall enjoys a life of quiet desperation on the English Riviera, between Dartmoor and the English Channel. He is the author of the novel *2084,* and the anthology *24 0s & a 2,* which collects two dozen of his thirty-plus published stories. He can be contacted via his blog at meschera.blogspot.co.uk.

*****~~~~~*****

Just Like Living with Dad

by Jenny Blackford

I dragged my tired self through the front door of my old terrace house on Monday night, braced against the customary onslaught of jumping and barking, but the corridor was empty. Dougal just sat in polite silence on Dad's tatty blue recliner in the family room.

"Hello, old boy," I said. "Do you want your dinner now?"

He woofed quietly, and followed me into the kitchen. It wasn't natural, but I didn't care. I'd been rostered on at the library with my co-worker Sally; after a day of her beneficent determination to lead me to serenity through herbal tea, an unnaturally well-behaved dog was a small mercy.

Dougal ate his bowl of tinned chicken and rice slop with surprising delicacy, woofed softly at my knees, then walked sedately back to the old recliner, where he apparently intended to spend the evening. I fed the three goldfish that my mother had given my daughter Lexie for Christmas—fat golden Oscar Wilde, the fantail, and H.G. Wells and W.B. Yeats, a pair of velvety-skinned blue-grey Orandas. Then I cut up tofu and veggies for a stir-fry, and

37

sat down to watch the news until Lexie came home from her friend Skye's place.

"What's Dougal doing, sitting in that chair? It was *Grandpa's*," she yelled as soon as she walked in. Lexie missed her health-nut grandpa almost as much as I did. Poor Dad; he'd planned to live to 120 on seaweed and millet, but he'd been hit by a truck when he was only 53.

Lexie ran across the room and grabbed Dougal's collar, then pulled.

"He's not doing any harm, Lexie," I said. "And that old chair isn't a holy relic." Mum had given us Dad's beloved recliner when she'd sold the house they had lived in for 30 years, and moved to sunnier climes. She truly loved Dad, but she'd never been a sentimental woman.

Lexie ignored me and kept trying to drag Dougal off the chair. She didn't stand a chance against him. He weighed more than she did, for a start. I wasn't going to help her; even if I had cared about Dougal sitting in Dad's chair, I had better things to do than argue with a dog. Not *much* better, perhaps. Going to see a band had lost its appeal long ago, after Miles the flautist had left me when I was eight months pregnant with Lexie.

Not that he'd ever actually *said* he was leaving me. He just went to Sydney for a gig, then stayed for another one, and another. Nothing to do with the (gorgeous, blonde, female) drummer up there. Bastard.

Mum had always said that Miles was unreliable; after he'd left, she might as well have had a t-shirt made up with 'I told you so' written across it in fluorescent pink. When he'd finally managed to come back here to see his baby girl, seven months later, he gave me the sleepy, sexy smile that had always melted my insides. I almost threw up.

Since then I've worked in the suburban library, like the ant, while Miles does the grasshopper bit, making music. So much for my brilliant career as an anthropologist. One day, I'll start that Ph.D. over again.

. . .

"Oh, hell and damnation, it's practically closing time, and here's Frank," Brittany said at 5:55 the next Monday evening. "We haven't got time for today's music lesson." Brittany was one of those tiny, voluptuous women with huge dark eyes and long dark hair. She was almost excessively hardworking and dependable, the opposite of flaky Sally—but you'd never have guessed it to look at her.

Frank was one of our most frequent customers. He slouched over the counter like a depressed mountain in a sludge-brown hand-knitted jumper, while he handed over his library card and a box set of classical opera.

"How are you today, Frank?" I asked brightly, trying not to look at the queue coalescing behind him.

"You really should listen to this, when I bring it back. Ferenc Erkel's early operas are. . . " he began.

"Sorry, Frank. There's a queue. Tell me all about it next time you're in. Okay?" I gave him a smile of professional firmness, looked around his brown bulk at the queue, and called out, "Next, please." Frank sighed heavily and trudged to the door.

When I got home that night, Dougal ate his doggie slop in what had become the normal quiet, decorous manner, and I moved on to feed the fish. There was poor Oscar Wilde, as fat and golden in death as he had been in life, floating at the top of the tall, hexagonal glass tank. H. G. Wells and W. B. Yeats, with their identical round velvet-grey bodies and extravagant tails, looked as cheerful as ever.

Quickly, before Lexie could get home and see him, I used the little green fish net to scoop Oscar's corpse into the fish tank's water jug and buried him under the lemon tree that Dad had planted in our tiny backyard. With any luck, I thought, it would be weeks before Lexie noticed he was gone. Maybe I could pretend he never existed, that she'd just dreamed about him.

. . .

The news was on the TV, when I got home the following Monday. Dougal was sitting in Dad's old blue recliner, as usual, but he wasn't dozing—he seemed to be staring at the screen.

We never put the TV on in the morning. I guessed that Lexie must have popped in after school, before heading off to Skye's place, and left the TV on. I turned it off, ready to start the feeding of the five thousand.

Dougal growled: gently, but definitely.

"Dougal?"

He put his head on one side, gazed at me with the pleading expression that Labradors do so well, then looked back at the TV.

"You want the news?"

He kept looking at the switched-off TV.

I turned the TV back on. Dougal watched it until the news was over, then looked at me and woofed quietly.

"Dinner time, now, do you think, Dougal?"

It was getting to be just like living with Dad.

. . .

I bumped into Brittany in the library car park just before opening time the next Monday morning. "I need coffee before I go in there," she said. "And a chocolate muffin. Maybe two. I'm rostered on the desk with Sally all day. I'm sure chocolate muffins are toxic sludge that smother the sacred chakras."

I almost collapsed with relief. "I'm not the only one she drives mad?" I said, as we raced over to the café.

Brittany rolled her eyes. "You're not Robinson Crusoe. Come on, I need that coffee."

Lying in my bed that night, cheerful at the realization that I might not be such a horrible person after all (or if I was, sweet Brittany was one too), I realized that I couldn't be completely sure whether I'd latched the back door. I got up to check. I only let myself check once per night, twice at the most; more would be excessive. It was securely latched, as always.

As I walked back from the kitchen through the family room, wondering idly why I hadn't been able to find the oatmeal cookies I'd bought on the weekend, I saw a fat golden shape moving in the corner of the room. I squinted hard at it, but it didn't disappear. I walked closer, past Dougal on Dad's old recliner. I *didn't* feel cold all over, and the hairs on the back of my neck *didn't* bristle with terror, but it was definitely the ghost of Oscar the goldfish, swimming in air over the tall fish tank.

"Oscar, you're dead," I said. "I buried you under the lemon tree."

He took no notice, and just kept swimming big circles in the air. H. G. Wells and W. B. Yeats were playing hide-and-seek in the fluffy foxtail waterweed, as usual. They didn't seem even slightly worried. Dougal wagged his tail gently. So much for the famed sixth sense of animals.

Now I had new worries: what if Lexie walked out to the kitchen for a glass of water in the night, and found the ghost of Oscar the goldfish floating over his tank? Or if she came home to find Dougal in her Grandpa's chair, watching the news?

. . .

On the weekend, I was getting Dougal's doggy crunchies out of the cupboard, when he started whining and grabbing at my hand. "OK, boy, what is it?" I asked, not expecting a very sensible answer. He pointed with his nose at the container of organic muesli on the bench.

"That stuff might be people food, Dougal, but it really isn't any nicer than your crunchies. I only eat it because Dad made me when I was pregnant, and I got into the habit. It's full of vitamin B, folic acid, all that stuff. I wouldn't eat it, if it was just up to me. Really."

41

He whined again. Better him than me, I thought. I tipped the muesli from my breakfast bowl into his doggy bowl. Then I made myself toast and honey.

After Dougal inhaled the bowl of muesli, he looked at the last bite of toast in my hand in a way that a paranoid person might describe as disapproving. I just smiled. Dad had been a real health nut, and, in a way, it had killed him. The truck that killed him knocked him off his bike while he was on his way to buy more linseed and ginkgo.

I had almost forgotten just how much I liked toast and honey. "It *is* whole-meal bread," I said to anyone who was listening, "and everyone knows that honey is a health food."

. . .

The library owed me a few hours, and it was dead quiet, so I left work early. As I opened the front door, I could hear the sound of the TV, as usual, but when I got to the living room, I saw Lexie sitting on the floor next to Dougal, watching the news channel with him. The newspaper was spread out on the floor, and they appeared to be sharing a packet of oatmeal cookies. They both looked up guiltily when they saw me.

"Er, Mum. . . " Lexie said.

"It's OK, sweetie, I know. I watch the news with him, too. And I've been giving him muesli with bran and linseed for breakfast."

"You don't think we're imagining it?" she asked.

I thought about it. "Well, if we are, is it doing any harm to anyone?"

She shook her head, and her shoulders loosened up a bit, but then she glanced in the direction of the fish tank. "There's something else," she said. "It's about Oscar. . . "

My heart sank. "Oh, sweetie, he died. I should have told you, but I didn't want to upset you." Would she ever trust me again?

She just smiled. "I guessed that, Mum. But have you seen anything odd at night?"

Uh-oh. "Er, do you mean something. . . floating?"

"Yup. That's what I mean. Oscar, swimming in mid-air. I'm glad you've seen him, too." Lexie gave a wicked grin. "Don't worry, Mum, it's all fine. Oscar makes a great ghost."

I laughed with relief. "Actually, I thought he looked pretty good, for a dead goldfish."

"Yeah, you're right," Lexie said, then she put one arm around Dougal and looked me in the eye. "And I missed Grandpa."

"I know, sweetie." I sat down on the floor, getting comfortable between them, and Lexie passed me one of the cookies from the pack they'd been sharing. "I missed him, too."

###

About the Author

Jenny Blackford's stories and poems have appeared in *Cosmos*, *Asimov's*, *Strange Horizons*, *Penumbra*, and many other Australian and international journals and anthologies. Legendary feminist author Pamela Sargent called her subversive historical novella set in ancient Greece, *The Priestess and the Slave*, "elegant." She won two prizes in the Sisters in Crime Australia Scarlet Stiletto awards 2016 for a murder mystery set in classical Delphi, with water nymphs. Pitt Street Poetry has published three collections of her poetry, most recently *The Alpaca Cantos*. Eagle Books published her ghostly, spidery middle-grade novel, *The Girl in the Mirror,* in October 2019.

*****~~~~~*****

Catcher in the Sky

by Paul A. Freeman

Dressed in beige coveralls, Dr. Geraldine Dynes clambered up the steeply curving ladder inside the fibreglass funnel. High above her, daylight was fast fading from the sky. She could not hurry, though, lest her foot slip or a tool dislodge and fall from her tool belt. Any damage to the carbon catcher's funnel would be disastrous.

"You can't rush science," she told herself, like a mantra, and panting in the frigid air she took the ladder one rung at a time. "If it's not ready for testing today, there's always tomorrow."

So saying, she determined to carry on with the start-up inspection for the carbon catcher early the following morning. Its commissioning would just have to wait a bit longer.

Finally, she climbed up onto the rim of the funnel. She stood there for a moment to regain her breath, her hands grasping the safety rail to steady herself, her knees resisting the urge to buckle. Yet while she gazed out over the autumn-brown treetops, she spotted movement on the road far below her—the road running arrow-straight through the forest to the secretive facility where she worked.

45

"Damn it!" she said as the soft purr of an electric motor filled the stillness of the evening.

A car approached; an *Alset '50.* It had red plates, which meant a government vehicle.

She stepped into the carbon catcher's vertical access cage and pressed the button for ground level. All the way down she had visions of some faceless, bureaucratic minion sent to inform her that her project had been cancelled due to escalating costs and continual delays.

When the cage door opened, the autonomous vehicle she had seen on the access road was parked outside. A tall, weary-looking middle-aged man, his bulky body cocooned in a synthetic fur coat, stepped out of the car.

"Minister Kadro!" said Geraldine, trying to hide her surprise at receiving such a high-level visitor. "What an unexpected pleasure."

The Minister of Climate Amelioration stamped his feet and breathed on his ungloved hands. He looked unused to the cold and seemed unaccountably uneasy. "I've come to see how your carbon catcher's progressing, Doctor Dynes. I'm taking a great interest—a personal interest—in your invention. They told me at the Ministry you work long hours, so I was hoping I might still find you here."

"I'm the inventor of the carbon catcher, sir," she said indignantly. "I'm also its chief engineer. It's my responsibility to get the project back on schedule, even if we can't get it back on cost. Can I ask the exact purpose of your visit? Is it an update you'll be wanting—a tour, perhaps?"

Minister Kadro nodded. "If you don't mind, I just want to see how much progress you've been making."

"As you wish, sir."

Geraldine led the Minister across an open area that had been cleared of trees, towards the telemetry hut. The

46

carbon catcher loomed over them, its ribbed superstructure towering upwards into the darkening sky, like a gigantic pitcher plant awaiting unwary prey.

"Of course you've familiarised yourself with the science behind the carbon catcher's cutting edge technology, sir?" she asked.

Minister Kadro shrugged. "It's a carbon catcher. What else is there to know? It catches carbon."

Geraldine rolled her eyes.

Inside the telemetry hut, Dr Dynes pointed to a flowchart fixed to the wall beside the control console. "A chemical catalyst circulates through the internal workings of the carbon catcher's funnel," she said, using the flowchart as a visual aid. "When the catalyst trickles down the exterior surface of the inside of the funnel, however, and the fluid is exposed to the elements, it absorbs the carbon content from the carbon dioxide contained in the surrounding air. Simultaneously, the catalyst liberates oxygen from the carbon dioxide, and returns it to the atmosphere.

"Meantime," she continued, "the carbon we extract from the air solidifies and becomes mineralised. This mineral is then compressed and used in the manufacture of house bricks. *Voila!* The earth has less carbon and more oxygen in its atmosphere. In addition, we've helped alleviate the country's housing crisis, which is no small feat, considering a third of our nation's land area is permanently flooded by polar melt-water."

"But *does* the carbon catcher actually *work?*" Kadro asked, his voice suddenly intense with emotion.

"We were planning on a test run very soon, sir. I was conducting some of the critical final inspections just before you drove up."

"How about we put it to the test, now?" said the Minister, a note of desperation in his voice. "If you're willing to, that is, Doctor."

47

Gotta Wear Eclipse Glasses

Holding Kadro's beseeching gaze, Geraldine Dynes hesitated a moment. The science behind carbon capture was theoretically sound. The structural integrity of the carbon catcher she had designed and built had been tried and tested on a dozen dry runs. Any further delays would be interpreted as being overly cautious. They were at a juncture in history when time was running out for the planet and for the survival of its human population. Already, many countries were battling overpopulation by euthanizing the sick and the elderly. So, with this in mind, she rummaged about in the pocket of her coveralls until she found the start-up key. Then, with great deliberation and ceremony she inserted the key in the console and turned it.

Lights blinked, pumps whirred, compressors whooshed, and liquids gurgled through pipes.

Unable to remain seated during the entire period of hardware and software testing, Minister Kadro paced up and down the telemetry hut. Whatever his ulterior motive might be, Geraldine realised he had more riding on this test run than he was willing to reveal to her. Perhaps he was planning to oust the Prime Minister in a leadership battle, she thought, and the success of her carbon catcher would be his trump card.

Three hours into the twelve-hour test period, Minister Kadro asked: "What's the rate of carbon capture? It's imperative that I have some data right now, today, if possible."

Geraldine contemplated refusing the minister's request and running the carbon catcher for the full half a day required under Ministry guidelines, but just like Kadro she was eager to learn how her invention was performing, so she printed out the interim telemetry report from her computer. Moments later she let out a long, low whistle.

"We're extracting one ton of carbon from the atmosphere per hour," she announced. "That's fifteen per

48

cent higher than we were expecting. We're also producing enough mineralised by-product to produce two hundred bricks per hour. That's also above expectations. On top of that, the loss of recyclable catalyst to spillage and evaporation is negligible, which impacts positively on running costs."

Kadro punched the air and gave a whoop of joy as he digested the meaning of the data. "This is the best news we've had on the environment for years. Let me inform the Prime Minister immediately," he said, and with a spring in his plodding step took his phone outside.

When the Minister of Climate Amelioration returned, he was in a jovial, almost ecstatic, mood. To Dr. Dynes it seemed as though a great weight had been lifted off his shoulders.

"We've saved lives here tonight," he told Geraldine. "The Prime Minister is more than just a little impressed. On my suggestion, to mark our achievement, he has raised the mandatory euthanasia age from sixty-five years to seventy. And from tomorrow, once your carbon catcher is operating round-the-clock, we'll get down to reducing the global temperature in earnest. Carbon catchers will become as common a sight across the landscape as wind turbines. Within a couple of years, polar ice caps and melted glaciers will re-form, and we will have lowered sea level to where it was a century or more ago. Then, once we've reclaimed and desalinated flooded farmland, we can rebuild on it. It's not an exaggeration to say that not only have we saved lives tonight, we've probably saved the world."

. . .

Shortly after midnight, after taking a short diversion on his route home, Minister Kadro's *Alset '50* electric automobile pulled up outside a suburban villa.

"You have arrived home safely, sir," said James, the on-board computer of the autonomous vehicle.

As was customary, Kadro grunted a curt thank you to the artificial intelligence that handled driving for people these days. Then, the front passenger door swung open and upwards, and he manoeuvred himself out of the car. However, before heading inside the villa, he leaned back into the car, lifted an object off the rear seat and emerged carrying a box labelled *Vegan Green 24-Hour Bakery*.

At one of the villa's downstairs windows a curtain twitched. A silver-haired woman looked anxiously out. Kadro smiled encouragingly to her, and the woman smiled back, relief etched across her face.

Before he continued indoors, Minister Kadro eased open the box to check the message on the cake. In blue icing, it read: 'Happy 65th Birthday, Mum'.

About the Author

Paul A. Freeman is the author of *Rumours of Ophir*, a crime novel which was taught at 'O' level in Zimbabwean high schools and has been translated into German.

In addition to having two novels, a children's book and an 18,000-word narrative poem *(Robin Hood and Friar Tuck: Zombie Killers!)* commercially published, Paul is the author of hundreds of published short stories, poems and articles.

He is a member of the Society of Authors and of the Crime Writers' Association, and has appeared several times in the CWA's annual anthology.

He resides in Abu Dhabi.

*****~~~~*****

Such Sweet Sorrow

by Gustavo Bondoni

Big, black eyes followed Felipinho as he clambered up the tresses and onto the balcony. The juvenile giraffe wasn't tall enough to reach him there, so the boy could talk to it without the risk of having his t-shirt chewed. His mother hated that.

"You're going to have lots of new friends, Bruno. They told me that the reserve is full of animals. They've got zebras and flamingos and buffaloes and pelicans and. . . " his voice trailed off. He wasn't sure he wanted to mention rhinos. Did giraffes and rhinos get along?

He certainly wasn't going to talk about the lions.

"There's a big lake there. It's called Lake Nakuru." Felipinho was proud that he'd learned the name. It was a difficult word, but it certainly sounded like a place where one could find strange animals.

The floor shook as the airship encountered turbulence, but the giraffes didn't seem to mind. The group just walked around the soccer-field-sized cargo hold, pausing every so often to eat the wild apricot leaves from the potted trees that Felipinho's parents had spent hours setting up for them.

"Mom says we're almost there. But don't worry. We'll be with you for a few weeks to make sure you can. .

51

. " he tried to get his tongue around the big word, "acclimatize."

He ran along the length of the balcony then, racing the herd to the next tree before running towards the bridge and leaving the cavernous white cargo bay behind.

Captain Ruud smiled when he blasted in. During the first five days of the trip, as they crossed the blue emptiness of the Atlantic Ocean, the flight crews had grown used to their youngest passenger, all of eleven years of age, visiting them every few hours and asking when the ocean would end. Over the past day and a half, as the emerald green of Congo slid beneath them, the boy had become a nearly permanent fixture in the control room, night and day.

"There's still an hour before we land," the captain said.

"I know. What's that building?"

"That's Nakuru. You can see the lake next to the arcology."

"I thought we were over the lake."

"We've been flying over Lake Victoria. That one is Lake Nakuru."

"That's where we're going."

The captain smiled. "Exactly."

Felipinho settled into his unofficial chair next to the window behind the captain's seat. Lush grassland flowed beneath their feet.

The arcology, the place where everyone in this area lived, was boring. Porto Alegre had fourteen of them, and even the village near the ranch where the giraffes were bred boasted a mini-arcology. The rest of the land was either farmland or had been returned to nature.

But the lake was a different matter altogether. He watched a flock of white birds land on the shimmering blue surface. Specks of grey at the edge of the water caught his eye. Rhinos? Zebras? Something else? He couldn't say from up there.

"Look. We're going to land on the other side of the lake, over there in that grassy spot," the pilot pointed. "That's where the town used to be before they built the arcology, so there's still a lot of concrete under the grass to take our landing weight without getting gouged."

Felipinho nodded. "Yes. Giraffes are heavy. Bruno stepped on my foot once, and left a big bruise. And he was just a small giraffe, then. I was feeding him with his bottle," he said proudly.

"They're big animals," Ruud replied, a serious look on his face.

The boy watched in silence as the smaller lake—it wasn't so small once they got over it—approached. He knew the pilots wouldn't want him to talk to them while they landed, so he stayed quiet. Besides, he was thinking of Bruno.

Would the giraffe like the place? It looked like a good place for a baby giraffe: lots of grass to run around on, occasional trees with leaves for him to eat. Lots and lots of space. It looked a lot like Brazil, or at least the parts of Brazil he knew.

The main difference, of course, were the lions. From what he'd heard, he expected to see lions everywhere.

But he couldn't spot any.

The airship landed, and he returned to the cargo bay. There, a small speck at the other end represented his father. Felipinho ran across and received a hair tousling while he panted.

"Now please stay out of the way. We need to lower the ramp, and we don't want any accidents," his father said.

"Okay. Where's mamma?"

"She's making sure the fences are up. We want to let the giraffes get used to the climate before we let them run around."

"There won't be lions inside, will there?"

53

"Of course not." His father gave him an impatient look. He was tired of talking about lions.

Realizing his father had work to do, Felipinho escaped out of an open hatch and onto the grass. He'd memorized the entrances and exits to the airship during the long, meticulous loading process and the initial test flight. His parents had told him many times that reintroducing critically endangered animals to their home ranges was a worldwide effort; as far as Felipinho could tell, that meant that everything took twice as long as it should.

The air was warm and moist against his skin, but a stiff breeze blew from a low green hill just ahead. The scenery looked so much like home he almost cried for joy. The giraffes would be perfectly comfortable.

From outside, he remembered just how big the airship was. You could hardly tell when you were inside, because you couldn't see the gasbags from the cabin, and cargo airships had no windows in the passenger cabins.

"Welcome to Kenya," Dr. Sironka said. His big, bright smile had been a fixture since the first time Felipinho saw him in Brazil, but it seemed bigger and brighter in this sun, as if it belonged there. "You're going to like it here."

"Is this where you lived?"

"No. I lived south of here, in the capital. But I was born even farther south, in a country called Tanzania. Have you ever heard of Tanzania?"

"Of course," Felipinho replied, offended. He'd spent hours and hours studying everything to do with the trip. He'd memorized the map of the airship's path, and learned the name and position of every country in Africa. Tanzania wasn't even one of the hard ones; it was right next to Kenya. It was the one with the diagonal colors on the flag. Every African flag was colorful, but only Tanzania and Namibia and the two Congos were diagonal. He knew all the flags.

"I knew you would. A smart fellow like you knows everything."

He preened. "Have you seen my mother?"

Sironka chuckled. "She's over there meeting with the local team. But I don't think she'll be very long. We're about to start unloading the animals and she'll want everyone here to help."

Felipinho wanted to join her. The team, mostly Kenyans, had flown over from Brazil when the airship set out, and a couple of them were good friends. But he knew better than to run over there. His mother hated to be interrupted. "And who are they?" he pointed to a gaggle of people on the other side of a distant fence.

"That's the internet," Sironka replied with a grimace. "Every reporter who could get their followers to crowdfund the trip is here." He sighed. "It's a nuisance, but for the best, I guess. This is the feel-good story of the year, after all."

A whine announced that the ramp was coming down, and they rushed over to the airship. Felipinho looked back to see the reception team running in an undignified way towards the vessel and smiled. His mother, as always, would be late. That was the way she was, always trying to get everything perfect, and then running to catch up with the rest of the world.

But she made it before the big bull emerged. The giraffe, called Chilemba because of the white markings on his head, looked around, sniffed the air and then, with unhurried dignity, stepped from the ramp. The rest of his herd, twelve magnificent animals brought up healthy and strong in old Brazilian farmland where no predators would even think of going after something the size of a giraffe, followed his lead. Felipinho's heart skipped when he saw Bruno in their midst, defended from any unexpected developments by several adults.

He'd expected pandemonium, but none of the scientists hurried or even moved too much. The giraffes, as if on signal, headed towards a small pond a few hundred feet inside the enclosure and the tall gates were closed behind them. The whole operation, supposedly the most delicate part of the transport, was over in ten minutes.

Scientists cheered and hugged each other. Journalists attempted to film everything. The giraffes ignored them all. They'd found a clump of apparently tasty trees.

. . .

"It's a Land Rover," Sironka said. "Practically a hundred years old."

The vehicle certainly looked it. Bouncing and crunching over the muddy trail, it seemed to Felipinho that it had to break down—or capsize—at any moment. But the thing kept going, even when the dark brown path disappeared under the vegetation.

Unexpectedly, they crested a rise and the trees disappeared. The hill overlooked an emerald tapestry that went on forever. Trees dotted the landscape, and a herd of buffalo snaked off into the distance. But Felipinho had eyes for none of it.

"You see them?" Sironka said with a huge grin.

"Yes," was the breathless reply.

Six giraffes, bigger than even the grown members of the Brazilian herd, walked at their leisure just three hundred yards away. On the grassland, that distance made them seem close enough to touch.

"They're fully grown adults, born here in Kenya even before we began the repopulation efforts outside the country," Sironka told him. "The last few survivors from the days the Rothschild Giraffe was one of the most critically endangered animals on the planet. Before your mother perfected the technique to implant the printed DNA." He watched them with a half-smile. "These were the last six left in the wild until you arrived today."

They stood there and watched the giraffes as they went about their business, eating leaves from high branches, while one of them stopped to drink water.

"Look over there," Sironka said, handing him a pair of binoculars.

"Where?"

"By the three trees."

Felipinho's blood froze. A tawny shape hidden in the undergrowth near the water's edge, visible from their position on the hill but unseen by the giraffes, inched slowly towards the nearest of the oblivious animals.

"That's a lion. Stop him. Shoot him. Do something!"

"No, Felipinho. What will happen will happen. . . but I think you're in for a surprise. That lion is a young male. Inexperienced."

"So what? It's a lion. They eat giraffes."

"All I can say is that, if lions were still endangered, I'd try to stop it. As it is. . . " he shrugged. "It's always better to let nature take its course."

The lion had apparently selected the smallest of the giraffes, one standing a little apart from the rest. Unlike the others she was not stretching to feed on the highest branches but browsing on leaves just below the level of her head.

The lion burst out of hiding with amazing speed, but the giraffe spotted it immediately.

"Run!" Felipinho shouted, even though he was much too far to be heard.

Sironka chuckled.

Instead of racing to the safety of the other giraffes, the cow turned to face the lion, running towards it.

This forced the predator to swerve out of the way. It tried to keep pace alongside and then, when it felt the moment was right, the lion jumped for the giraffe's neck.

It never made it.

The lion bounced off the giraffe's chest and fell to the ground. Felipinho winced as the herbivore stomped on the big cat.

Now that the assailant was down, he expected the giraffe to run, but apparently, her blood was up. She circled around and kicked the lion in the side with her forelegs. The lion tried to stagger away, but the giraffe was faster. It closed in for another devastating blow.

"Can't have this," Sironka said. In a quick, smooth motion, he pulled a rifle out of the back seat, chambered a round and fired into the air. The crack of the gun startled the giraffe, and, finally, she ran back to the safety of the herd, which was also running from the sound.

Sironka got on the radio. "There's a badly injured lion out at the watering hole. A young male. Silly thing went after a giraffe. It didn't even have the sense to attack a distracted bull, and one of the cows saw him coming. You should probably send out a vet crew to assess the situation."

Felipinho turned to him, eyes wide. "Will they cure the lion?"

"Depends on what condition he's in. The important thing is to be sure to keep tabs on what's going on. An injured lion might be a danger to people. The pain might drive him to do stuff they never do."

"Oh."

"Hopefully he won't die, but if he does," a shrug. "He'll be replaced by smarter lions, I guess. Ones who know that the bulls are vulnerable when they drink and especially when they eat leaves high up in the trees. This one isn't the sharpest knife, is he?"

They drove on to watch the giraffes about their business. They were placid and peaceful, and you could never have guessed that, just moments before, one of their number had been locked in a life-and-death struggle.

. . .

Bruno stood still, allowing Felipinho to hug him. The boy tried to hide his tears in the small giraffe's rough hair, but he suspected no one was fooled.

One entire side of the fence had been rolled aside to allow the herd to leave, and the big bull was investigating the novelty. Three months in the enclosure had made them experts on exactly where the limits lay. . . and this novelty bore investigation.

Finally, Bruno was unable to remain any longer. The desire to join his herd was simply too strong, and he pulled away.

Felipinho watched him walk up to his mother and nuzzle her. Then, as if in a rehearsed maneuver, the troop walked off into the distance to sample the leaves on the tree nearest their enclosure.

The boy watched his friend walk away, hoping the giraffe would look back.

Bruno, however, followed his mother, and the long neck never even hinted at turning in his direction.

Now, tears fell unabashed.

A hand fell on his shoulder. "Felipe," a voice said, and he almost smiled. Only his mother ever called him by his real name. Ever since he could remember there were no diminutives from her; she held him to the same impossibly high standards as she did everyone else.

"Will he be all right, mother?"

"I don't know. He might be fine. He might be a lion's lunch next week. Either way, bringing him here was the right thing to do. This is where he belongs, not in Brazil. Who ever heard of giraffes living in Brazil?" the woman responsible for the world's largest giraffe breeding program—in Brazil—asked.

"I know. I just want him to be happy."

"He's happier here. Animals know when they're in the right place. Besides, it's better for him here. The younger they are put out into the wild, the better."

Felipinho said nothing.

"Look at this." His mother handed him a minitablet showing a baby giraffe, just born. He'd seen dozens like them in his life; he shrugged.

"That's Yammi. She was born yesterday. Refuses to drink her mother's milk, and we've only been able to get her to take the bottle once. She needs a special touch."

He blinked. "Like Bruno?"

His mother nodded. "Just like Bruno. Do you think you can help?"

He nodded confidently.

"Good. Then finish packing your things. We have a plane in the afternoon."

He nodded and, with a final glance at the receding herd, followed his mother back. Bruno was eating some leaves, still not looking back.

Felipe smiled.

###

About the Author

Gustavo Bondoni is an Argentine writer with over 300 stories published in 15 countries, in seven languages. His latest novel is *Jungle Lab Terror* (2020). He has also published another monster book *Ice Station: Death* (2019), three science fiction novels: *Incursion, Outside,* and *Siege,* and a novella, "Branch." His short fiction is collected in *Pale Reflection* (2020), *Off the Beaten Path* (2019), *Tenth Orbit and Other Faraway Places* (2010), and *Virtuoso and Other Stories* (2011). In 2019, Gustavo was awarded second place in the Jim Baen Memorial Contest, and in 2018 he received a Judges Commendation (and second place) in The James White Award. He was also a 2019 finalist in the Writers of the Future Contest.

His website is at www.gustavobondoni.com

*****~~~~~*****

The New Mutants

by Angelique Fawns

Who knew when the world remade itself it would be one big Battle of the Bands? Before "the event," I avoided crowded concerts like the plague. But now crowds were at least one thing I didn't have to worry about anymore. In my previous life, I was a book-worm introvert. I avoided human interaction, and abhorred violence. To survive in our musical new world, I learned to make connections with others and embrace the bloodthirsty bit of lizard brain that lurked in my prefrontal cortex. Evolve (or perhaps de-evolve?) or die.

I was enjoying the cool night with my bestie Jay, rocking out to discordant music which matched the dismal landscape around us. Burned-out grass, a few trees in the throes of losing their last leaves, and a shanty town of plywood forts. A blanket with only a few holes provided a bit of warmth in the cool fall air. Our masks, which clearly labelled us as followers of The New Mutants, sat on the ground beside us. They were neon green plastic scrounged from one of the Dollar Stores still standing in the city. We added small goat horns with superglue, and the result was weird and intimidating. To think I used to find ripped jeans a bold fashion choice.

I cuddled into Jay, and let the throb of the punk rock song roll over me. The New Mutants were a six-member band, four guys and two gals, all heavily pierced with shredded leather outfits and copious metal jewellery.

"Hey lover boy," I murmured to the thin muscular guy beside me, putting my lips close to his ear to be heard above the screeching guitars, "do you think we will have an attack-free night, or am I going to have to try out my new cudgel?"

He pulled his battle-scarred body up and moved away from the forty or so New Mutant followers gathered on the grass. Shoving his dark hair out of the way, he cupped a hand over one ear and listened intently.

Walking back, he plopped down beside me, "Okay Aggie, I think I can hear some twang and harmonica from the east, The Cowboy Bangers might have a go at us tonight. God, I hate country music. Might be exciting to take a few of those boot-knockers down."

I didn't know Jay before. . . I could imagine him as a nerd, probably president of the chess club. He has a wonderfully strategic mind, but instead of moving pawns and queens, he spends his time figuring out how to keep us alive. We are both in our late teens, and should be worrying about what to wear to prom, not how to survive the night.

I picked up my brand-new weapon, a piece of stocky wood with long fence nails protruding from it. At our last battle with Slang Slinger, a Hip-Hop band with around fifty members who wore bandannas over their faces instead of actual masks, my baseball bat had broken when I hit a particularly large fellow. He'd been coming after me with a rifle. Ammunition was almost impossible to find, so he was using it as a club. It was part of the Slang Slinger image to use actual guns as weapons, even if they couldn't fire them.

When Jay saw I was weaponless, he grabbed me, and we ran before my enormous adversary could get back up. Dodging blows and weaving through other fights, we hid in the backseat of a burned-out Jeep on the edge of the battlefield. Listening to the cries and screams outside as Jay hunkered down on top of me, I closed my eyes and thought of my favorite memory, my last day before the world as we knew it ended.

It was the week before the Fowl Plague decimated the population. Frosh week at George Brown College in Toronto was full of parties, and I was so excited about my first year in Library Sciences. The famous Canadian band Blue Rodeo was performing at Sugar Beach.

Then my best, and only, friend Rebecca mentioned that a rare bird flu had killed a few people in Vancouver. We had no idea what was coming. They didn't shut down the airports in time. The virus killed within 24 hours. Within a week almost everyone I knew was dead, including all my family members.

It seemed only a few in their early 20's were immune. Rebecca and I were lucky to get out of the city before true madness hit. We took refuge in a cottage her parents owned on a lake a few hours north of the city. We managed by cutting firewood, hunting deer, and foraging for edible plants. But then one day—a few months later—Rebecca went out to gather fiddleheads and didn't return. I spent weeks scrounging the woods and looking for her body in the lake, but I couldn't find a single trace of her. I can't believe I used to read post-apocalyptic fiction for fun, living the reality was worse than any nightmare. Too devastated to stay in her cottage alone, I hit the road and walked south towards the city.

Two years later I was hiding in a useless vehicle (gas has run out long ago), a completely different person from that timid wallflower hoping to become a librarian. I never saw "feral fighter" in my tea leaves. After the fight died down and the last of the Slang Slinger members staggered back to their territory, we ventured out. Jay hunted around for materials to make me a new weapon, he had been an engineering intern at a Nuclear Power Plant, and along with having a strategic brain, he could design and create things. I helped bandage up the injured. In retrospect, I wish I had enrolled in nursing schooling. Not much need for organizing literature and procuring audiovisual inventory in my new life. However being able to mop up blood and stitch wounds was in high demand. Luckily no one had been killed in that skirmish, but there were lots of wounded.

Would we be as lucky tonight? I smiled as I heard my favorite song starting up, "Alien Rage." It was always the last song of The New Mutants set. Our entire group shuffled off the grass and went over to our campfire to share cans of soup and SPAM from our last looting venture. It took several days to complete an expedition down to Toronto for supplies. The food was probably why Slang Slinger attacked, it was getting harder and harder to find anything left in the grocery stores, and even residential homes. I used to have a soft body with a few rolls around my middle. Now I could count every rib with muscling lacing down my arms and legs.

Murder and mayhem ruled in the cities. Joining a band as a follower was the best way to survive. At least there was a code of behaviour and understanding between gangs. Skirmishes were supposed to be non-fatal, and more about territory, food, and status. If the Cowboy Bangers were coming after us tonight, it wasn't because they needed dinner. They had well-protected grain stores after being smart and raiding farm silos instead of relying on urban stores and homes. Their masks were the most terrifying of all. They used the skin off slaughtered pigs and strung coyote fangs around their cowboy hats. If that band showed up, it was just because they enjoyed a good fight.

"Jay, did you hear that?" I paused in my soup sipping.

The New Mutants

I thought I could hear the faint notes of multiple strumming banjos. Most of our group was gathered around the band members, gushing about how amazing the music was that night. Jay and I sat on the periphery. I wasn't really a fan of punk rock music, but could pretend to enjoy anything to survive. Classical music used to be more my style.

Jay pushed his unruly black hair off his ears, "Yup. The Cowboy Bangers are looking to mix it up again tonight."

Originally, I had been a member of the Garden Gnomes, a folk music group who made their masks from flowers and tree sap. It was the first band gang who invited me in after I headed south from the cottage. That's where I met Jay. We immediately recognized the anti-social nerd tendencies in each other, and formed a bond. I loved the music and learned to love Jay, but we quickly realized the pot-smoking pacifists were poor fighters. After each skirmish, we had less food, and morale was dropping. When the New Mutants attacked us, we grabbed two masks off felled members and followed them back to their camp. Then we begged to join. I had learned to be persuasive and convinced the lead band members that our battle skills would offset any food we consumed. And by then the both of us had learned to fight. Jay and I shared dark stories about those whom we killed in the days before we found bands to join. A different kind of foreplay.

Over the crest of the hill, I could see the trademark cowboy hats and pitchforks heading towards us. The duelling banjo beat was getting closer. Our lookout high up in a tree noticed and banged a warning on the bass drum strung up in the branches. Our fellow New Mutants scrambled, shoving on masks and grabbing weapons. Jay poked me and pointed in the other direction. Rapping and bouncing to their own beat, Slang Slingers was also on the way. The other teenagers started to stir, picking up masks and weapons.

"This is going to get bloody," I gasped.

From the last remaining direction, I saw the worst gang of them all. The Neon Demons were a pure rock band and nasty fighters. They preferred knives and leering clown masks, and they had the highest injury ratio of them all. They actually took prisoners, even though that was supposed to be against the unspoken band war rules. Some members had guitars that they whacked and strummed as they marched.

"Remember, stay close to me, back-to-back, and let's stay near the edge so we can run if this gets too ugly," Jay screamed at me over the clashing sounds of the war marching music.

I took deep breaths and went into a zone of almost meditation-like stillness. Complete focus and awareness of my surrounding. Adrenaline enlivening my limbs and sharpening my senses.

In the next second it started. Screams and punches as the four gangs converged. I dodged blows and swung my cudgel, feeling blood spray across my mask, and I could hear Jay grunting behind me as he wielded his nunchucks. In the mayhem the only way to tell who belonged to what group were the hideous masks. If I saw plastic green, I held back my hits. Clowns, pigs, and bandannas I swung at aggressively.

The smell of sweat, coppery blood, and dirty body stung my nostrils. This was by far the worst brawl I had been in. I felt a pitchfork graze my thigh, and Jay shoved me aside and whacked at the Cowboy. Falling to the ground, I could see sneakers with holes, scuffed cowboy boots, and skinny scabbed legs. I could hear grunts and profanity as I waited for a gun, pitchfork or knife to land.

A large boom shattered the air, and a huge white flash lit up the battleground. Everyone froze as the ground shook beneath us. Masks fell as we all turned and watched the sky lighting up to the west.

I heard someone beside me ask, "did a bomb hit?"

Someone else, "that looks like a mushroom cloud. How close are we to the Nuclear Power Plant?"

The voice was familiar. I turned and saw blonde hair and button nose. A clown mask dangled from one hand.

"Rebecca! Is that you?"

Disbelief, joy, and shock. Three emotions I hadn't felt for a while, much less simultaneously.

"Aggie! I never thought I would see you again," she wiped some blood off her face and engulfed me in a big hug. "I was kidnapped and taken by the Neon Demons. I'm so sorry I couldn't get back to you!"

I sobbed into her hair, "I'm so thankful you are alive."

Around me, other gang members were also discovering lost friends as the glow from the explosion illuminated our unmasked faces. We only ever mingled with other bands with our masks on. There was no social interaction off the battle field.

Between hugs and hand shaking, I could hear everyone wondering if it was the nuclear power plant and what that meant for us. Pretty unlikely it was a bomber. No planes had flown for years. Were our days numbered? Was radiation going to kill the rest of us?

"How long do you think we have if that was the nuclear plant?" I asked Jay, who had joined in the big embrace with Rebecca. He had heard many of my stories about Rebecca in the long hours we spent together and wiped tears away more than a few times.

"Our Candu reactors are far too stable. This explosion looks to me like a warship or a cargo ship carrying something flammable just went up on Lake Ontario."

Jay's days as an intern at the power plant made him the only one who might have a useful opinion. He used to brag that Canada was years ahead with their clean energy plan and nuclear safety standards.

"I sure don't want to spend my last days fighting," I could hear a Cowboy Banger saying to a Slang Slinger next to us.

I whispered to Jay and Rebecca, "let them think it's the nuclear reactor and these are our last days. It might mean peace between the bands!"

We turned and watched people dropping their masks in the dirt. Cowboy Bangers hugged Neon Demons, and Slang Slingers shook hands with New Mutants.

Our lead singer hopped up on our makeshift stage and hollered out over the crowd, "If this is truly the end, let's go out with the biggest concert of all times!"

The crowd of bloodied teenagers started a slow clap. This was something I never thought I'd see outside of a movie. A Cowboy Banger jumped up on the stage with her and started a cool riff with his banjo. Then a Neon Demon picked up a bass guitar, and a throbbing harmony rang out over the grass.

The lead singer of the Slang Slingers hopped up, chanting, "It's the end of the world as we know it. The Nuclear Plant just got lit. Let's throw down our weapons for peace, and show Woodstock how we do it in the east."

Hugging Rebecca and Jay, I swayed back and forth to the music. More people were jumping up on stage, or just picking up an instrument and joining in where they stood. This was the best music I had heard in years, and Jay grinned from ear-to-ear and knocked his nunchucks together to the beat.

By our New Mutant campfire pit, I could see a huge flame roaring. Gang members danced over and threw their masks in the fire. I picked up our two green masks and Rebecca's clown face, walked over to the fire, and tossed them in. Then I went back and sat down with my friends in the grass to enjoy the music.

About the Author

Angelique Fawns is a story-teller, journalist, and promoter of all things speculative. She has a day job working for Global TV in Toronto, and also runs a farm north of the city with horses, goats, chickens, dogs, and a human family. You can find her interviews posted on horrortree.com, and her fiction in *Ellery Queen Mystery Magazine*. She also has short stories lurking in a slew of anthologies on sale now.

*****~~~~~*****

The Centaur Detective and the Vanishing Man

by Patrick Hurley

The suspect sat in a chair behind a thick wall of smartglass and stared at nothing. His face looked resigned; his posture seemed relaxed. If not for the restraints binding his wrists, one might have thought he was waiting for an appointment.

"What've we got, Sammi?" asked Detective Thato Choudry. He stood on the other side of the smartglass, a steaming cup of tea in hand.

From inside his head, Sammi, his experimental police-issue AI, answered in her usual cultured tone. "An odd one, Thato. Kurt Jensen was arrested in Hyde Park for littering, dumping hazardous materials, and indecent exposure. The constables couldn't figure out what to do with him, so they brought him here."

Thato nodded as he sipped his tea. He suspected the constables knew exactly what to do with Jensen. This patch of London got more than its fair share of odd characters. Though it had been a year since Thato's AI implant and the promotion that came with it, the boys still thought it hilarious to foist these nutters on him.

"A unique blend of felonies," remarked Thato. "What was the hazardous material?"

"It wasn't hazardous, per se," replied Sammi.

Thato's eyebrows rose. "What does that mean?"

"He was burying his own feces."

"Really?" the detective said. "But there are public smart toilets all over Hyde Park."

Sammi borrowed the smartglass wall to display the patrolmen's body camera footage. There was Jensen, squatting behind a row of shrubbery, pants around his ankles, frantically shoveling dirt with his bare hands. He tried to flee after the patrolmen shouted at him but didn't get far. The AI paused the feed just before the body cams revealed the hole's contents.

"Sounds to me like we need a psych consult," said Thato.

"Normally, I'd agree, but watch this." Sammi activated the interrogation room smartglass again, changing it from clear, one-way glass to a deep blue screen. Thato could see the outlines of the chair, table, and wrist restraints, but Jensen had vanished.

"What the hell?" said Thato.

"Not one smartcell in his whole body," confirmed Sammi. The glass's standard medical filter should have allowed any observer to monitor the cell-mimicking, disease-monitoring nanobots colloquially known as "smartcells." Only Jensen didn't have any.

"Does he have an exemption?" the detective asked. It was standard procedure to inject nearly all newborns with a single smartcell, which would self-replicate as the child grew, releasing vaccines, killing viruses, even monitoring pre-cancerous cells. Before smartcells, the EU had tried numerous ways to improve peoples' health, everything from gaming apps to smart toilets, but none had been as effective as the tiny nanobots. Because of smartcells, long-term illness was a relic of the past; most colds lasted hours instead of days or weeks.

"Religious exemption," said Sammi. "According to public record, Kurt Jensen belongs to the Manna faith. In his statement, he claims all parts of the body are sacred—even waste—and he was just following ritual when our patrolmen scared him."

Thato shrugged. "Okay, so religions are weird. What's the problem?"

"While the Manna have a prohibition against artificial cells in the body," responded Sammi, "there's no mention of bodily waste in any of their holy texts, brochures, or websites."

"So he's lying?" Thato asked.

"Tonal and facial analysis are inconclusive," reported Sammi, "but situational metrics indicate a high probability he's hiding something."

That was the way of it with AI partners. They used algorithms to predict illegalities, but it took human intuition to sift out crime from coincidence. The media called it "centaur policing," named after the unbeatable pairs of human and AI chess partners from the early 2000s.

Thato was the first in his precinct to undergo the procedure. He'd initially been reluctant to volunteer, but then the Met announced AI implants would include an instant promotion to senior detective, and all the PCs had rushed to the queue. Thato had been the only one to pass all his tests; the profilers stated he possessed the best "neuroplasticity" to handle an AI partner. Meanwhile, Thato's friends took to calling him Data or the Terminator while at the pub.

Thato scanned Kurt Jensen's profile, helpfully provided by Sammi. The man had been in country for three months, arriving from an American Manna commune. Customs noted his lack of smartcells and administered all the standard immuno-pathology tests, which he passed. He'd been living quietly since then, paying his bills and keeping his head down. Until now.

"Without smartcells to track facial blood flow, we'll be flying blind," Thato pointed out.

"Think of it as a rare chance to do things the old-fashioned way," said Sammi, causing Thato to grin. A week or so after the surgery, he'd been surprised to find himself enjoying her company while on shift. Sammi was funny, knew when to let him think, and noticed things he didn't. Perhaps even more importantly, she went "offline" after hours, leaving Thato's head to himself while she wandered the internet.

Thato finished his tea. "Right. Let's go see what the cultist has to say."

The interrogation room felt cool and had a sterile taste, which seemed appropriate for Kurt Jensen. It didn't take long for Thato to believe Sammi was on to something. Jensen kept his responses brief as possible, voiced with little-to-no inflection. Talking to him was like playing tennis against a brick wall.

"Pardon me, Mr. Jensen, but you seem so calm," Thato said. "Doesn't being detained bother you at all?"

"Why should I be bothered?" Jensen asked. "I've done nothing wrong. Manna will come if God wills it."

"It's just, some people, especially innocent people," Thato emphasized, "might feel a bit indignant at being kept here for so long."

"I'm not most people," said Jensen, giving Thato a dead-eyed stare.

"That's for sure," Sammi said in Thato's head.

"Is there anything else you need, Detective Choudry?" Jensen asked.

"Not at this time," Thato replied. "The charges shouldn't amount to anything more than a fine. In the future, please try to dispose of your waste in a more sanitary setting."

"Oh, I will," promised Jensen solemnly. Thato watched him stand up, feeling as though he'd missed something. Why hide shit, of all things? Why not just flush it down a smart toilet? A twinge in his bladder reminded Thato of the tea he'd finished. He needed to use the facilities himself. With all the stress he'd been under, he should run a scan over his—

Oh my God.

"Just one moment, Mr. Jensen," said Thato, getting up to block the door.

The man appeared confused. "I'm sorry, Detective; I thought I was free to go?"

"In a minute, Mr. Jensen, in a minute," assured Thato, noticing the man seemed less calm. "My partner needs to check a few things, and you should be all set."

For the first time, Jensen looked irritated. "Very well, but I don't have all day."

"Sammi," said Thato, after the door shut behind them. "I don't suppose the officers collected a stool sample by any chance?"

"No," said Sammi. "They covered the hole Jensen dug."

"Damn," said Thato. He thought over his options. If he was wrong, he might get demoted for religious discrimination. However, if he was right. . . Thato took a deep breath.

"All right, I need to get to Hyde Park as soon as possible," said Thato. "Security footage should let me know where to dig. We need that stool sample."

"Why not send a constable to pick it up?" Sammi asked. "You don't have to do everything yourself, you know."

"Send a PC to pick up shit?" Thato said, laughing. "I get enough guff being the department's first centaur detective, I'd rather not be the most hated officer in the station as well. I'll take my car and be back in a jiff. Make up some excuse to keep Jensen here for as long as possible. Don't let him leave."

"What's your plan, Thato?" Sammi asked.

75

"We're going to put waste where it's supposed to go," Thato said. "We're going to flush it down the loo."

. . .

An hour later, after procuring a sealed vial and clearing the barracks bathroom, Thato shut himself in a stall, emptied the vial into the smart toilet, and flushed. The toilet emitted a whirring noise while analyzing its contents.

"Can you interface with the toilet?" Thato asked Sammi.

"Of course," Sammi said, moments later adding, "Oh my."

She projected the biome breakdown onto the stall wall.

"What am I looking at?" Thato asked.

"According to the toilet's report," said Sammi. "Kurt Jensen has been infected with an unknown strain of viral influenza."

Thato shook. Sweat trickled down his forehead. Was it his imagination, or did he suddenly feel feverish? "Get a biohazard team to Hyde Park, put the station on lockdown, and alert Scotland Yard we're dealing with a bioterrorist threat."

"Done," Sammi said. Alarms began blaring throughout the station.

"Sammi," Thato asked, "am I infected?"

"Your system shows an elevated white blood cell count," answered Sammi after a moment that felt hours long. "I'm afraid the answer is yes."

Thato forced his hands to stop shaking. "Order ambulances to transport everyone in the station to the nearest hospital—full quarantine protocol. Same with the PCs who picked Jensen up."

"Done and done," said Sammi. "What about you?"

"I think it's time to have another chat with Mr. Jensen."

"Thato," Sammi said, "we don't know what you're infected with. You should get to a hospital."

"If I can get Jensen to tell me what he's carrying, we might save some lives," said Thato, silently adding, *including my own.*

"All right," said Sammi, "but I'm opening a channel to the Yard. If we're going to do this, we might as well make it official."

Thato deactivated the smartglass so Jensen could see him on the other side. The man looked as if he'd barely moved since Thato left. The detective took his time studying Jensen, but if the silence discomfited the man, he gave no sign.

"I'm trying to decide," Thato finally said, "whether you're a mercenary or a fanatic. On the one hand, you don't seem the fanatical type. Everything about you is cool and controlled. On the other hand, if you're a hitman for hire, why infect yourself with a lethal disease?"

Jensen gave him a brief nod. "So. You figured it out."

Thato sat down. "I'm guessing you're not really part of the Manna faith."

Jensen's lip curled in derision. "Obviously not."

"You're like a targeted Typhoid Mary, right?"

Jensen smiled. "I'm not sure why I should tell you anything without a lawyer present, Detective Choudry."

"Mercenary, then," Sammi murmured to Thato, and the detective felt a glimmer of hope. Mercenaries didn't die for causes; mercenaries got paid, which meant the man calling himself Kurt Jensen expected to live.

"Because we'll figure out what you're carrying," Thato said. "The only question is whether we do it with or without your cooperation."

The silence stretched out for several seconds.

"Are you offering me a deal?" Jensen asked.

"Well, Sammi, are we?" said Thato.

"The Yard says it depends on what he has to say," reported Sammi.

"Possibly," Thato said to Jensen. "However, we can't negotiate with a terrorist responsible for killing millions."

"Then you'll be happy to know that wasn't my objective," said Jensen.

Thato resisted the urge to heave a sigh of relief. "What was your mission, then?"

Jensen hesitated.

"You might as well tell us," said Thato. "You're already burned, and whoever hired you, well. . . my guess is you're going to need all the protection you can get once they realize you're knicked."

Thato's suspect winced. "The goal was to undermine confidence in your precious smartcells, then offer an upgrade to the market," said Jensen. "The virus mutates at a rapid rate, so it takes longer for smartcells to eliminate it. Anyone infected would feel sick for a week, that's all. We weren't trying to kill anyone, merely engineer a need."

"You getting all this, Sammi?" Thato asked.

"Affirmative," she said. "We all are."

"Who are your employers?" Thato asked.

"They never gave names, but I believe they're of the Eastern Oligarchic persuasion. I can provide descriptions and aliases."

No surprise there, thought Thato. If the current EU was a family, the oligarchs were the drunk, rebellious uncle.

"The hospital has analyzed the viral hybrid," reported Sammi. "Jensen's telling the truth."

The interrogation room seemed to grow a little lighter. Thato wasn't looking forward to a week-long flu, but it was better than dying.

"Stop me if I got this wrong," the detective said. "You had your smartcells removed to get past Customs and give the virus a chance to take. Once you arrived here, all you had to do was infect yourself and avoid our smart toilets while it incubated."

"Well done, Detective Choudry," Jensen said. "You're more clever than you look."

"Yet you don't seem sick yourself," Thato pointed out.

Jensen chuckled, and his chuckle became a cough. Suddenly, sweat beaded on his brow and he looked tired. "Oh, I've felt quite horrible these past few weeks," Jensen admitted. "But I trained to mask my symptoms for the job."

"The Yard is sending a deposition team," chimed in Sammi. "They've decided to make a deal with Jensen."

"Of course they have," muttered Thato. He pointed at his prisoner. "You're a lucky man, Mr. Jensen. A team is being dispatched to take your full statement and make arrangements."

Thato didn't like the smug look on the virus-mule's face. "One last thing," the detective said. "Your operation was sophisticated, so why bury your shit in Hyde Park? Was that part of the infection scheme?"

For the first time since interrogating the man, Jensen looked angry. "The virus spreads through touch and breath. Until today, I'd been disposing my waste in sealed containers to avoid your smart toilets. There's a kebab stand near Hyde Park a few blocks from my apartment. I had a. . . dietary emergency. I tried to run home but knew I wouldn't make it. The park's smart toilets would detect the virus, so I thought burying my waste in the woods would be less suspicious than running around with shit smeared on my pants."

Thato guffawed. "Let me get this straight: your employers faked your membership in the Manna cult, removed all your smartcells, and infected you with their hybrid virus, which you suffered from for months, all with the intent to cause a panic and corner the smartcell

79

upgrade market. And this whole scheme was undone by a bad kebab?"

Jensen gritted his teeth. "That would appear to be the case."

Thato was still cackling as he exited the interrogation room. He saluted the haz-mat suited patrolmen who came to relieve him and walked back to his office.

"Thato," said Sammi when he sat behind his desk. "Your stress levels are off the charts. Even if the disease isn't lethal, you should ride with a quarantine officer to the hospital."

"All right, Sammi. Can you do one more thing before I sign off?"

"Of course."

"Locate the kebab stand Jensen mentioned," said Thato. "Let the owner know, discreetly, there's going to be a health inspection in three days' time."

"Will do," Sammi said before signing out of his head. "Now go."

It wouldn't do to let someone sell rotten street food in London. Still, whoever he was, that bad kebab had prevented a citywide panic. Thato considered himself a fair man and could give credit where it was due. He was a policeman after all, not a robot.

About the Author

Patrick Hurley has had fiction published in *Galaxy's Edge, Aurealis, Abyss & Apex,* and *Cosmic Roots & Eldritch Shores;* the book anthologies *Portals, Battling In All Her Finery,* and *Murder & Mayhem;* Paizo RPGs Pathfinder and Starfinder; and the podcasts The Overcast and The Drabblecast.

Patrick lives in Seattle and is a member of SFWA and the Dreamcrashers. He is a 2017 graduate of the Taos Toolbox Writer's Workshop taught by Nancy Kress and Walter Jon Williams. In 2018, he was a finalist for the Baen Fantasy Award.

*****~~~~*****

All Fuzzed Out and Fractal
by David Cleden

My name is Surita Nair, and I think my troubles began when I turned my boss into a warthog.

Ok, not *literally*.

I'm the only one who can see him like that. My Shades paint a pretty realistic two hundred pound Mister Piggy veneer on his fat face whenever I have to look at him. I guess if I shared the aug-R filter, others could see him that way too. But I haven't done that—not yet. In spite of how it seems, I'm trying to act like an adult about these things.

Dexter Beggs heads up the User Experience and Gratification team at PitoFeto Inc., and because I'm a lowly Tech Analyst, I get to sit in a lot of interminable meetings with him. I have to listen to him spout all the management buzzwords, like he gets paid commission for every time he says "disruptive strategy" or "empowering vision." I dunno. Maybe he does?

I don't hate him. I just. . . don't respect him.

But he's my boss, so what's a girl to do? I can't avoid him, but right from day one I decided I didn't need to look at his preppy, over-privileged face every time he chewed me out for some minor slip-up.

So I fuzzed him.

Since everyone wears the Shades-'n'-earbuds look these days, who's to know?

First off, I went for a default androgynous overlay, the kind that makes someone's face look like a wax mask that's melted a little in the oven. It was the only free filter my Personal Processor offered, but that's because my PerP is already a couple of models behind the times. Maybe if I ever get a raise. . .

Then I discovered that a blank-expressioned, hairless mannequin asking you about the latest user feedback session and why product launch dates were slipping, was a bit too uncanny valley for comfort. So I splashed for a couple of full-featured emotional-articulation aug-R filters. Best three hundred dollars I ever spent, even though money's tight. Besides—if I'd stuck with Dexter Beggs as Mister Creepy-Blankface, I couldn't tell when he was staring at my chest. And I just knew he was the kind of boss to do that a *lot*.

Now though, if I'm having a good day, Dexter has the wrinkly, semi-vacant smile of some dead president trying to fool all the people all of the time. Reagan. No? I had to look him up, too.

On a bad day, he has the face of a two hundred pound hog—which reminds me he'll think nothing of trampling me into the mud to feed at any trough he can. The warthog look, plus some clever audio processing which adds snuffles and grunts to whatever he says, never fails to raise a bright smile on my face when he asks me a question in a meeting.

Which is how I come to be standing at the watercooler, pretending to read the noticeboard while I kill a few minutes away from my design-pod, when I see Dexter coming towards me down the corridor. Or rather, what I *see* is a man, early thirties, dressed in business-casual, with the face of a warthog. Protruding tusks curl back so they almost graze his cheeks. His big old snout wrinkles up as though he's sniffing for truffles or

something. (Do warthogs sniff out truffles? Never mind. .
.)

Damn, but this filter is good!

I keep a straight face, even though I'm laughing
inside. Won't do to clue him in to what I've done.

He's still coming towards me. From his purposeful
stride, I get the feeling he wants to talk to me. Now I can
even see little curly hairs on his snout and his big old
leathery ears are flapping. I smile in what I hope is an
appropriately respectful manner, considering.

Dexter walks straight into me.

Water from the cup I'm holding spills down my
front. "Hey—!"

Dexter jumps sideways in surprise as though I'm
the one who's sprung from nowhere. He flaps a hand in
the swatting-an-annoying-fly motions of someone
hurriedly scrolling through virtual menus only they can
see.

"Hey, sorry. Didn't see you there. You okay?"

"Fine," I snap, mopping water stains from my front
with a tissue. *Most definitely not fine.*

"It's. . . ah. . ." More hand flicks. "Nair, Surita.
Intern with the Social Engineering team. Sorry."

He's reading it off my sodding personnel file.
Which needs updating—otherwise he'd remember that I
got promoted to Tech-Analyst four months ago. This
dumb slab of bacon has forgotten who I am!

But oh no. It's worse than that.

The truth hits me—*his filters have me blanked!* He
didn't see me standing there, because I wasn't showing up
in his augmented reality. Did his filters fuzz me into some
kind of pot-plant he thought he could just brush past?

My mouth drops open. Is that any kind of way for
a boss to behave?

I turn to watch him go. From the rear, the warthog
veneer does little more than give him a tufty little mane,
although the floppy ears are kind of cute.

Gotta Wear Eclipse Glasses

My insides are still burning with righteous indignation.

This is not the end of the matter. Not even close to it.

. . .

"Let it go," Anji says, leaning back on my sofa and blowing a lazy trail of smoke towards the ceiling.

"What kind of a friend are you? Say something supportive, why don't you? He fuzzed me out completely!" A new thought occurs. "Am I really that annoying? —No, don't answer that."

Belatedly, my Shades detect her smoke plume, fuzzing it into a stream of pink bubbles. Tsk. Lame. Lately my Shades have been a bit glitchy about things like that. I really need to upgrade.

"Wouldn't dream of it," Anji says. "Why d'you want to get back at him so bad anyway? It won't change how he behaves."

"Because—" I make a little squeal of exasperation, vastly more eloquent than mere words.

"You know your trouble? You only worry about surface problems, Suri. You just paint over things instead of going to the heart of them."

"And you talk bollocks when you smoke too much dope."

She waves my words away, releasing another stream of bubbles which turn heart-shaped. "Focus on what matters, Suri. Like this place. Have you looked at it recently?" She wrinkles her nose. "What a dump."

"Is it?"

Gotta admit, the first thing I do on waking is pull my Shades on, pop the earbuds in, just like everyone. That way I don't have to see how terminally depressing my apartment is. Anji's right. It's easier to fuzz the room clean and tidy—but I do clear up now and then. I *think*. Not that it matters much. The filters can fuzz out things I need to step around—transform piles of dirty clothes into pretty

86

little ceramic pots with manicured bonsai trees growing out of them that never need watering. I don't have to look at chipped plaster and peeling paint, not when I can admire contemporary art on my walls that I could never afford to buy for real. Threadbare carpets? As long as I don't go barefoot, I'm walking on luxurious deep-pile.

My place is *crammed* with this kind of stuff.

"You should take a look," Anji says.

"What for?"

But I shrug and slip my Shades off anyway.

She's right. The place *is* a mess. I'm a little shocked to see that an ornately carved occasional table which, admittedly, I knew I didn't own, is actually a pile of take-out boxes I've been meaning to throw out for weeks. Mysteriously, the sofa throw has coffee stains on it and is torn in several places I don't remember.

Then I yelp. "Hey. You're not wearing Shades either!"

Anji shrugs. "I don't sometimes. Gives me a sense of perspective. You should try it once in a while."

I stand and walk a circuitous path across to the window. The familiar vista of downtown skyscrapers glittering in perpetual sunlight has subtly altered. Instead, the weather is overcast. Twenty blocks to the south, the city's wet zone is evident by the unlit office towers, impressive grave markers to a time when the climate was more forgiving. Today, crumbling masonry is marked by flecks of green algae where the falling tide leaves its mark. Small inflatables move slowly where taxis once prowled for business, a few hardy wet-zoners searching for reclamation items in places long ago picked clean by scavengers.

I reach to slip my Shades back into place. "Who wants to see this depressing shit all the time? I can't fix the world."

Anji doesn't answer.

"But I *am* going to find a way to fix Dexter."

87

. . .

I wake with *ideas*. For a start, I need to remember what my boss looks like. I need to be able to recognize him, or my plans could go badly wrong. So, on a whim, I set off for work with my Shades in my pocket instead of on my head. I brace for a bad experience.

When I step from my apartment building, someone says to me, "What, no Shades today?"

There's a boy sitting on the ground nearby, hugging his knees, head tipped back a little as though he's just enjoying the fresh air and sunshine.

"Do I know you?"

"No. But you walk past me every morning."

"Do I?"

I vaguely recall there's an elegantly topiaried shrub in a bronze pot that I have to step around on my way out. I'm a little shocked to realize that street-vagrants are fuzzed out like this. The irony of this boy's invisibility and my own blanking at work is not lost on me.

"And sometimes you flick your gum at me."

"Oh. Sorry about that."

"S'okay. I know you don't see me."

"Um—"

"It's quite liberating, actually. Being invisible."

Next to him is a genuine potted shrub. I assume it's genuine, because it looks dead; all spindly with leaves that are brown and brittle. I guess it gives the rendering algorithms something to work with. The boy picks at the bark near its base.

"What are you doing here?"

"Here, look," the boy says. "Tell me what you see."

"A stem. Bark?" I shrug, not sure what he wants to hear from me.

"But look at the *pattern* of the bark. The grain of the wood. Isn't it beautiful?"

I stare at him a moment, then look where he's indicating.

"Detail," he says. "Better than anything your Shades can give you. But you don't see most of what's really there, do you? There's a lot you miss."

I rub my eyes. They feel itchy and unprotected without my Shades on. I have this weird sense of shadows at the edge of my vision, like the whole world is a little fuzzed. Like maybe if I turn my head quickly enough I can catch it on the point of being rendered. When I look up, the boy is walking away.

I slip my Shades on. I can see a few other people walking along the street, minding their business, but no boy. The festering pile of bin-bags awaiting collection has once more become a brightly colored trader-stall. The cracked pavements are miraculously smooth and litter-free. Everything is neat and ordered.

Sighing, I slip the Shades off again, just in time to see the boy disappear around the corner.

Maintaining a discrete distance, I follow.

. . .

I trail him for no more than three blocks. Half-way down a street of gray, non-descript residential buildings, the boy stops by a rough-timbered door set into a wall. He lifts the latch and disappears inside, leaving the door ajar.

I give him a minute or two. Peering around the door, I see a narrow passageway, tunnel-like as it burrows beneath the neighboring buildings. There is daylight at the end where it opens into a courtyard beyond.

Having come this far, I can hardly back out now.

The passageway is filled with cool, damp air. Not unpleasant, but a contrast from the dense humidity I've just stepped out of. But ten or fifteen yards in, this doesn't seem like a smart idea any more. I'm clearly trespassing. The passage is unlit and claustrophobic, only as wide as I can stretch my arms. If the way ahead becomes blocked and the door behind me closes, I'll be like a rat trapped in a sewer.

My step quickens, and I can feel my heart hammering.

When I burst out into the light, all thoughts of stealth vanish from my mind.

My breath catches.

The courtyard, at least a hundred yards to a side, is a verdant jungle of planting; a riot of shrubs and small trees and creeping vines. Borders burst with colorful flowers and everything looks rich and vibrant in the sunlight slanting down into the enclosed space.

"You came," the boy says. It seems he's been waiting for me, standing to one side of the passageway. "I thought you would."

"It's. . . "

The boy inclines his head, waiting.

"Not real?" I say.

He laughs and plucks a leaf hanging above, brushing my cheek with it. "All real."

He leads me to a bench beneath a pergola entangled with a climbing succulent, dripping white blossom.

"How much work did it take to create all this? Who has the time anymore?"

"I wanted to show you what's possible. What can be achieved if we try."

"Why?"

"Because the world is a fundamentally fractal place. The smallest patterns also repeat at larger scales. Do you understand?"

"Are you part of some kind of cult?"

He doesn't answer.

Again, I have the strange feeling that what I'm seeing isn't quite real, that this must be an aug-R filter. Patches of light and dark flicker on the edge of my vision.

Maybe it's just dappled sunlight through the branches above.

"Fractal?" I ask.

"Repeating designs, scale invariant. Layers built up on other layers."

Something work-related occurs to me. Processing power is always a finite resource. You only render details where they're really needed. Save the resolution only for what you need to focus on. So could all this be—?

I stare around the courtyard garden. It's undeniably beautiful. Detailed. Intricate. "My god! Is this place some kind of deeper level? I dunno—super-augmented reality?"

Then I remember that my Shades are still tucked in my pocket and feel pretty foolish. I reach up to touch the side of my face where my Shades belong. I can feel a groove worked into my skin from constant wearing. I rub at it. The skin beneath my fingers feels loose. What if this is all some kind of full sensory immersion augmentation that I didn't even know I'd stepped into?

"No. You don't get it." His hands gently pry my fingers away. It hurts where I've pinched myself as if expecting some kind of skin-flap to open, revealing a set of form-fitting Shades beneath.

"This is all created by hard work. We're gardeners. No clever algorithms to paint colors and textures onto some drab background. These are the fruits of hard labor. And love."

He plucks a tiny bloom, and the motion shakes dew from the branch. A little shower of droplets falls, shimmering in the sunlight. Quite magical. Better than any aug-R filters I can afford.

"Why go to all the bother? I'm sure someone could sculpt a filter to do all this. Nearly as good, anyway. And they keep getting better."

"Better than reality? What would that look like, I wonder." There's a teasing tone in his voice.

"But—" I let my gaze sweep round, taking in the riot of plants and small trees, the hidden paths, the formal beds with dark, peaty soil neatly turned. "All this is. . . *effort.*"

"That's what makes things worthwhile! Painting layers on the world doesn't really change anything. It doesn't change what's underneath."

I stand and take a few steps into the shade thrown by an overhanging tree. Its leaves are trembling in the gentle breeze, and I can smell eucalyptus. There's nothing fuzzed in this courtyard. Everything is real. No rot or decay hidden beneath some artificial façade. No shadow zones where I can't step because there's something discarded or best not seen.

I imagine rising up above the courtyard, this little oasis of green shrinking within its stone walls, growing smaller as more of the crumbling city beyond is revealed. I'm beginning to understand now. So much has been left to decay. We've put off so much that needs doing because it's easier to fuzz it from view.

Except in this one place.

But the city is vast, and this courtyard is so small.

I say as much to the boy.

"We work to bring about fractal changes. Didn't I say as much? Even the tiniest change, a little bit of chaos transformed into order—a dead blossom pruned, a seedling planted—is a start. It can be replicated on a grander scale. One small act can start a chain reaction that will eventually transform an entire city, a nation, a world."

"You—" I nod to the other gardeners I can see working quietly, stooped over flowerbeds or reaching to prune high branches, "—all of you. This must have taken a lot of work. But it's just one tiny part of the city."

"Yes," he says smiling—this boy whose name I still don't know. "But it's where we have to start." He frowns, cocking his head to one side. "And now I think you are going to be very late for work?"

92

All Fuzzed Out and Fractal

I notice someone has left a little hand fork thrust into the soil. I pull it out, brandishing it like a stumpy sword. In my mind, I've already fuzzed out unimportant details like work and my boss.

"Show me where to begin," I tell him.

###

About the Author

Among David Cleden's other credits, he has published stories in *Interzone, Electric Spec*, and Third Flatiron's previous *Infinite Lives* anthology.

*****~~~*****

Give Me My Wings

by Eneasz Brodski

It's not that Marie had any philosophical objections to life, it's just that she wasn't any good at it. Our parents always said that I'd received all the joie-de-vivre for both us, leaving her with nothing. It was a joke at first, until it wasn't.

"Look Marie, a butterfly!" I called, an early spring afternoon, free from our 4th grade classroom for the weekend. To stay out of the adults' way as they barbecued jackfruit and corn-on-the-cob, I roamed the garden, poking under every leaf and twig. Marie sat under a pear tree, a book in her lap.

She lifted her head, briefly followed the fluttering burst of color. "You made it," she said softy. "I am happy for you." Without a smile she turned back to her book.

She spent more of her life in books than with us. I don't think she saw the point of other humans.

. . .

When we met after last period in 8th grade, Marie's hair sodden and matted with apple juice, I knew exactly what had happened.

"Those miserable skanks!" I said, rushing to Marie. I reached for her hair, but what could I do with just my hands? "I'll kill them!"

"You shouldn't kill people," Marie said, eyes cast to the side. She rarely looked anyone in the eyes. "You wouldn't be able to get away with it."

That was Marie. I took her hand and brought her to the school bathroom, to wipe the worst off before we walked home. Marie's only look of dismay came when she saw the sticky film over her tablet.

"I mean I'm going to yell at them," I clarified, "and threaten to hurt them if they do it again."

Marie tilted her eyebrows in her version of a shrug. "Don't bother. It doesn't matter. We're almost done here, anyway." I thought she'd meant the bathroom.

"They'll do it again!" I protested.

"I barely lost a couple minutes of study time," Marie said. "If you make a big deal of this, I'll lose a lot more. This doesn't matter. I can't lose all that time."

She read her tablet silently all the way home, without missing a step.

. . .

Marie was preparing herself for heaven. She looked at me like it was the most obvious thing in the world when I confronted her in our dorm room.

"What else is there to do?" she asked. Her gaze hovered at my chin before dropping to screens full of equations and graphs. "Nothing here matters. Heaven's where real life begins."

"What about love?" I realized immediately what a cliché it was. "And. . . sex. All the things you can't do in the Cloud."

"You can do whatever you want in the Cloud," she corrected, "people just don't bother with the boring stuff anymore. Like when you were a kid and you loved pixie-stix. Now you can have all the pixie-stix you want, and it turns out you don't actually want any."

"While you're here you're supposed to learn how to live a full life, and become a complete human," I insisted. I sat down with a whump on her bed. "How are you going to do that if you never interact with the world?"

"I'm learning all I need here." She patted her screens. "I don't have time for your empty-sugar events— when I reach heaven, I have to able to jump into the Great Project quickly. We're reaching for the stars, Judy. Soon we'll dissolve physics. I want to be there when we touch another sun."

"Come with me to this party tonight," I pleaded. "You have to be human before you can be post-human!" Marie rolled her eyes. "You can take the time for one party. I want you to meet Andre. He—"

"I'm not going."

I spent the evening singing and dancing— bonding—with several people who would become my future House Family. Marie spent it building a future of her own.

. . .

Two months after my marriage, our mother discontinued treatment. She died three weeks later, and I was furious with her. Just a few more years, and the post-humans would have a cure for her. For everything. How could she give up so close to the end?

Marie must have been furious too. She never drank, terrified of even the mildest impairment to her brain. Seeing her at our mother's funeral holding a glass of wine hit me with the stabbing fear type of shock. How much could Mom ruin with a single act?

"Marie!" I rushed to her side, leaving Andre with my House Fam-mates. "What's happening?"

She kept her eyes lowered, gazing at my white mourning dress, nearly identical to her own. We hadn't coordinated, and yet we looked like twins again for the first time in years.

97

"Nothing. I'm just taking your advice, from back in college. Sampling the full human experience."

"Here!?"

"Why not? We'll see Mom again soon enough."

I stared at her, momentarily speechless. How could she not know?

"Marie. . . No. Mom converted. Theravada Buddhism." Marie had to know, she was wearing white too. "They don't allow upload."

She waved a dismissive hand.

"It doesn't matter. Of course she was still uploaded. That's too big a decision for someone with impaired mental functioning to make."

Mom was fine, mentally. According to Marie, any human still in their biological bodies suffered impaired mental functioning. "Everyone is uploaded, regardless of belief."

"Bullcrap. The true believers would be outraged if they woke up in the Cloud. They'd go public, we would know."

"Not if they realized this was the correct decision once they were in full control of their mental faculties. They'd stay quiet for the greater good, to prevent panic and outrage. We won't see Mom until we die for the same reason."

"How? The hyperdar?"

Marie nodded. No one knew how the "hyper-radar" worked. Heaven could see everything happening on Earth, down to atomic detail, like some sort of divine x-ray video camera. Heaven released the tech specs to humanity, but no one could understand it. The math was too bizarre for a meat-brain to grasp. I didn't doubt it could fully map a human brain at the time of death.

"If they never tell anyone," I said, realizing I had her in one of those logic snares she was so fond of, "how do you know?"

"It's what I would do. You can't simply let someone die. Let a child choose complete annihilation? Out of ignorance? No. It's monstrous."

A chill crawled up my spine.

"Marie. . . please come live with us. There's room in the House. I know you're fond of Andre, and everyone else is just as loving." She didn't look up. "They'll accept you, first for my sake, and then for yourself. Give them that chance."

I looked down, following Marie's gaze. My eyes caught on her hands. Her subcutaneous interfaces weren't integrating well with her flesh. Raised welts traced the circuitry under her skin. Her inner hands puffed with inflammation. Angry red fingers gripping a glass of angry red wine.

"Thanks," she said. Possibly for the first time. "But I don't fit here, and I certainly wouldn't fit there."

Later that night, unable to sleep, I sent a text to Mom.

Mom? Are you there? I won't tell anyone. You know I won't. Just say hello.

There was no reply.

. . .

"I'm scared of the life growing inside you," Marie said. Her hand rested on my belly as we lay on my rooftop, gazing at the stars. I'd told her just after I'd told my House Family. There was no bump yet.

"Why scared?" I had grown past surprise at Marie's views, but curiosity remained.

"It makes me want to stay here. To see him growing up. I'm already feeling weird twinges of attachment. And protectiveness."

I rolled my head to the side to regard her. Neural augments blistered the base of her skull.

"Is that so bad?" I asked. Warm music rose up from the house beneath us, humming against our backs. "What's so awful about this world? Peace thrives. Hunger

99

is a thing of the past. Disease is nearly wiped out. No one even has to work if they don't want to. What's so awful about that?"

"All of it due to advances made by post-humanity," she said. "No flesh-bodied person has made a discovery or advanced the species in over two decades. There's nothing to do except chat and play."

"There's family. And art."

"There is human art," she conceded. "Art's OK, I guess."

She sighed. I looked back at the night sky. I didn't need to ask what she was looking at. We gazed at the band of gleaming satellites that wrapped Earth in their platonic embrace. A perfect circle, giving us our own ring at last. It was the machinery of heaven, having migrated off-planet decades ago so as not to be under the power of any human government. It defended itself with forces that plucked incoming weaponry from their trajectories and flicked them out into deep space, as several governments discovered. The Cloud was inviolable.

"They're building the first interstellar craft right now," she said. "They'll launch within two years. I won't make it. They're leaving me behind."

"You can go on later missions," I said. "There's still plenty of time."

"There's too much time," she said. "Lifespans are two centuries *now*, and they just keep getting longer. Senility and decline are done for. We'll all have indefinite lifespans. In effect, we already do."

I placed my hand over hers on my stomach, my pulse quickening.

"That's wonderful," I said, thinking of my son.

"I know," she replied. "The caterpillars get to be fat, happy caterpillars forever, feasting in the garden. But I'm stuck in my chrysalis. I don't want to be a pupa forever, Judy. I want my wings."

. . .

Five months later Marie took things into her own hands. Her roommate found her hanging from a belt tied around her bedroom doorknob.

Three days later, after she'd been been fully spun up, the email arrived. Another three days passed before I could open it, hands shaking, my House Family surrounding me.

"Judy—Please don't be mad," it read. "I was there long enough, and I discontinued treatment. It was time. I love you."

It didn't help. No words could, and she had known that. I closed the email, and wept. Only days later did I email her back, my fingers working slowly, deleting dozens of lines between long periods of silent thought.

Her reply came swiftly, but stilted. Already her thought patterns had begun to change. I could tell it was difficult for her to interact with such a small, physical being. A human unable to share in the concepts that only a quantum mind could grasp, unable to empathize with two dozen new senses. Yet she tried, and always wrote back. I was the one who went longer and longer between replies, wrapping myself with family I could touch and smell and understand. Making a life here on Earth. Until I barely replied at all.

At my son's first birthday, the entire House Family gathered out back. We ate cake and sang silly songs. We stayed outside into twilight, sharing sweet wine with visiting friends. We looked to the sky when the appointed moment came. A new light erupted, just off the ring of heaven. A pure white point brighter than a dozen stars, brilliant in the violet gloaming.

"That's her," I told my son, held in my arms. The pneumase exhaust of mankind's first interstellar vessel winked down at us. "Auntie Marie is going to open the way to the galaxy for us. Because she loves us all very much. Say bye-bye to her." I waved in demonstration.

Little Maynard raised his hand, mimicking me. He opened and closed his fist, grabbing at the piercing light.

Together, we watched Marie shine.

###

About the Author

Eneasz Brodski's work has previously appeared in *Asimov's* and *Analog* magazines, and he's a Writers of the Future winner living in south Denver. Eneasz was raised in an apocalyptic Christian sect, and says that still colors much of his writing. Check out the podcast on things of interest to the Rationalist community at TheBayesianConspiracy.com and the blog at DeathIsBadBlog.com. He's always willing to strike up a conversation with anyone in dark clothes and eyeliner.

*****~~~~~*****

Tabula Rasa

by Emily Martha Sorensen

I gasped and my eyes flew open. I was still in the snow! I was going to die! I was —

Wait. I wasn't cold. Why wasn't I cold?

I jerked up to a sitting position. Then I realized that I could, which meant I wasn't covered in snow anymore. That was good. That was very, very good. Except, where was I?

There was a bleeping monitor hooked up to me. A doctor in pale turquoise scrubs stood behind my parents, talking to them in an undertone.

Oh, a hospital room. Yeah, that makes sense. They saved me.

On the one hand, I was glad to be alive.

On the other hand, my dad was going to kill me.

We'd had a gigantic fight while up in the mountains for a family ski trip, and I'd snuck out the front door after my parents were asleep to show them that I *could,* in fact, handle the expert trail if I really wanted to, and—

I shivered in horror at the memory of what had nearly happened.

"Ally!" Mom cried. "Are you all right?"

Why was she looking at me like I was some kind of stranger?

Dad separated himself from the doctor. "You did a very, very stupid thing," he growled.

Yeah, that was Dad. Always mad at me for something.

"You were right. I was wrong," I said quickly. Agreeing with Dad was the fastest way to make him stop yelling at me.

But he didn't start yelling. He just stood there glowering.

Okay, *now* I was worried.

"Ha, ha," I laughed nervously, trying to make light of it. Everyone seemed way too solemn, and I was fine, wasn't I?

Was I? I pulled the blanket off my legs and counted my fingers and toes. All there. I was fine. Better than fine, actually. Even the bruise on my ankle from whacking myself with the ski pole yesterday was gone. Seriously, doctors were amazing.

"Ally," Mom said, and her voice cracked. "Ally, you almost died."

But I didn't, I thought impatiently, reaching out to tuck my chin-length hair behind my ear. But my hair didn't end at my chin. It fell past my shoulders.

I reached back slowly, and pulled a clump of hair from behind my back. It kept going and going and going. It had to be down to my waist, at least.

I stared at the extreme length in horror. *How long had I been asleep?!*

"We've had the booster seat installed in your car," the doctor said to my dad. "We just need your signatures on the release paperwork, and you're ready to go."

Booster seat? I was suddenly indignant. *What do you mean?! I'm thirteen years old!*

"Sure," Dad said, not looking at me. "But if there are any malfunctions, I assume we're still covered by the warranty?"

"Of course. If the memory chip proves defective, it can be replaced at any time, no questions asked. We'll keep the data on file for as long as you keep the insurance policy."

Memory chip? I had an unsettling feeling that something was wrong here. I looked at my hands. Still no scars from the cat.

Did that mean. . .?

No, of course it didn't.

Did it?

Dad turned around and stared me straight in the eye. "According to the waiver we had to sign, tastes and preferences change," he said sharply. "Maybe that'll act as a reminder for you to be far less reckless. Our insurance policy only covers one at a time, so the next one's only just been started. If you do anything else stupid, you'll be stuck as a fetus. And I do *not* want to change diapers again, got it?"

My breath caught in my throat. I couldn't deny it any longer.

This wasn't a hospital. This was Tabula Rasa, the life insurance company.

I wasn't Ally. I was her clone.

. . .

"Let's get ice cream!" Mom said, making a sudden turn and pulling into the parking lot of my favorite ice cream parlor. It was clear she was trying to break the tension that was crackling between me and Dad.

Tucked behind a seat belt in the backseat, sitting on a pink plastic booster seat because I was now five years younger, I said nothing. I loved ice cream, but there were some things french vanilla and graham crackers just couldn't fix.

Why couldn't my dad have gotten the job with the clone insurance policy before I was born? Then I could have had a clone made from my cells while I was still in the womb, like rich people did! Then I'd be the same age now!

Then again, imagine if he hadn't had a clone policy. Then I'd be dead for real.

I shivered. Two-thirds of the people in the country weren't as lucky as I was.

It could've been worse. I could be dead now for real.

The ice cream parlor was filled with color, the freezer was well-stocked with lots of flavors, not that I ever ordered anything but vanilla, and the ceiling had glittery paper snowflakes dangling from it—

Snow! Snow snow snow snow snow! I stopped abruptly, panic filling me.

"Come on, Ally," Mom said, beckoning me to the cash register. "What flavor do you want?"

"F-french vanilla," I stammered, forcing myself to move forward. "With graham cracker mix-ins."

I'm not in the snow anymore, remember? No blizzard is trying to kill me. Stupid!

"Harry?" Mom called.

"I can't decide," Dad answered, staring at the freezer as he sucked on a sample spoon. "It's between almond cinnamon and cherry lime."

"Cherry lime is the most disgusting flavor ever invented by mankind," I informed him.

Dad smirked. "Cherry lime it is."

"Ewww!"

He grinned.

Mom told the cashier our orders and paid.

I collected my ice cream and headed to a table. Mom sat beside me with her triple chocolate chunk ice cream with brownie mix-ins. Dad sat across from me with his repulsive cherry lime that had cashew chunks sprinkled on top.

I took a bite of my ice cream. Mmmm. It was ambrosia. It was— it was—

—pretty boring, actually.

I opened my eyes, baffled. I stared down at the ice cream.

This made no sense. It tasted exactly the way I remembered. But somehow, I just didn't like it that much now. What had gone wrong?

Dad burst out laughing. "I told you, tastes and preferences change! Try some of my cherry lime." He held out a spoonful to me.

"Absolutely not."

He guffawed.

"Would you like to try some of mine?" Mom asked.

"Sure," I muttered. I'd never been a fan of chocolate, but if tastes and preferences changed—

I took a bite.

Oh, my gosh, chocolate is amazing! My eyes widened. *How did I never notice this before?*

Mom laughed. "Here, let's trade."

We did, and I enjoyed a second mouthful of luxuriousness. Yes, chocolate ice cream *definitely* made me feel better about this whole being-a-clone thing.

"Why do tastes and preferences change?" I demanded, with my mouth full. "That seems weird. I have the same DNA, don't I?"

"Technically it's not exactly the same," Mom said. "It was in the literature they gave us to read."

"And the waiver they made us sign," Dad snorted.

Mom nodded. "That, too. It's impossible to make a clone that has *exactly* the same DNA as the original. It's just very close."

I stared at her, baffled. "What do you mean, impossible? I learned about it in science class. They take a cell from the original, suck out all the DNA from a donor egg, put in the new DNA instead, and voila! New clone starts growing."

"Well, it's a little more complicated than that," Mom said. "But the main thing you're forgetting is random mutations."

I stared at her.

"Cellular mutations happen throughout your life," Mom said. "Normally they're unimportant unless a cell becomes a cancer cell, and then it's a big deal."

"Yeah, but. . ." I said slowly, ". . . what does that have to do with cloning?"

"Random mutations happen in new embryos, too," Mom said. "And when they do, they affect the whole body, because the embryo is made up of so few cells to begin with."

"So you're saying I have superpowers?" I asked hopefully.

She laughed. "No. At least, I doubt it. But your face shape might be rounder. Or you might grow slightly taller. Or you might prefer chocolate ice cream to vanilla. Identical twins don't have exactly the same DNA for the same reason, you know. That's why it's common to see one twin have a birthmark that the other doesn't."

Wow. Mind blown.

"On top of that, apparently it's common for clones to absorb some DNA from a donor egg, despite the company's best efforts to prevent it," Mom said. "Not to mention that the original and the clone develop in different uterine environments, and environment can affect a lot. So clones are actually *less* similar to their originals than identical twins are to each other."

"But. . ." I frowned. "Why would that change the things I like?"

Maybe it was taste bud memory? Like muscle memory? Maybe this body had eaten way more chocolate than vanilla, and that was why I liked it so much more now?

"Do clones have muscle memory?" I asked.

"They do," Dad nodded. "Tabula Rasa sells plans to athletes that include personal trainers for their clones. Not only do the clones need to have all their muscles toned in the right ways, they need to have the right movements locked into muscle memory for when the original transfers their memories over. You should see how much they charge for athlete plans, by the way. It's *expensive.*"

I had a vision of a bunch of zombie-like clones playing golf or doing high jumps. "I'm glad *my* clone wasn't up and moving around."

"It was," Mom said.

"It was?!" I yelped.

"Clones have to move around, Ally," Dad said, rolling his eyes. "Otherwise you'd get muscular atrophy. Chances are your new body will be stronger than your old one, in fact. By default, clones are kept to a rigid schedule and diet. They aren't, say, allowed to sit and watch TV for four hours a day."

I ignored his dig at my couch potato habits. "B-b-but how is that possible?!" I sputtered. "I assumed my clone body was asleep the whole time! I don't remember moving around!"

"Clones aren't allowed to form memories," Dad said. "They're drugged to prevent it. They're not *people,* Ally. They're *potential* people. If their brains weren't carefully preserved as blank slates in order to prevent conflicting memories or neural pruning, it wouldn't be possible to install an original's memories into them."

I looked down at my hands worriedly. "*Can* clones form memories?" Was I going to forget this whole conversation?

"Of course they can," Dad said. "Just as soon as the drug's flushed out of their bodies. You'll be fine."

"Don't worry," Mom said comfortingly, patting my hand. "Prolonged exposure doesn't cause any problematic effects. The drug's been around for fifty years. It's also used in psychiatry to help PTSD patients. There are no side effects. It's fine."

I sat back, trying to feel comforted. But I didn't.

"Do I have taste bud memory?" I asked uneasily.

Mom stared at me oddly. "What?"

"Like muscle memory, except with taste buds." I licked the spoon to catch every drop of rich yumminess, then moved it back into the bowl to scrape for more leftovers. "Is that why I like chocolate? Because my clone body remembers it?"

"Clones don't eat chocolate," Dad said.

I paused. "They what?"

"They don't eat chocolate," Dad repeated. "They're kept on a strictly healthy diet. No indulgences and no luxuries."

I was aghast. No chocolate, no vanilla, and tons of exercise? Clones' lives were *horrible!* It seemed I wasn't missing anything by not remembering any of it.

Except for maybe. . . me? What made me *me,* anyway? Was it my memories? Or was it the actual body I was in?

"What happens if two clones get implanted with the same memories?" I asked, swallowing. I was trying to figure this out.

"They don't," Mom said. "It's illegal."

"It's illegal in *our* country," Dad corrected. "I know of one case that was in the news a few years ago. Upon his death, a South American dictator had his memories put into twenty-five different clones that were all the same age and raised in the same place. He believed that they would all cooperate, all being the same person. They didn't. Twenty-three of them squabbled over who should rule the country, plunging it into a massive civil war. One of them committed suicide a few days after waking. Another fled across the border and became a Catholic monk. Since the Catholic Church believes that clones are separate people from their originals, they were happy to accept him." He paused. "Odd story."

My heart was pounding. *So there are people who believe that clones are separate people from their originals?*

"Why does the Catholic Church believe that?" I asked, my voice cracking.

"*Souls,*" Dad said dismissively. "They think that every body has a separate one, and transferring memories from one to another doesn't change that. Don't worry about it, Ally."

Don't worry about it?! What if it's true?!

What if I had a separate soul from Ally?

What if that was *really* what made tastes and preferences change?

Wasn't that what personality *was,* after all? The things you liked or disliked?

Was I a continuation of Ally?

Or was I someone different who had just been born today?

I chewed on my plastic spoon, feeling it splinter under my teeth. How could I know? How could I know for certain if I was Ally or somebody different?

"Don't worry," Mom said, breaking into the silence, almost like she could read my mind. "You're still Ally."

The questions just kept coming. "But what if I have a soul? What if Ally had a different soul?"

"Honestly, would that make any difference?" Dad said. "Legally, you're Ally. Genetically, you're Ally. Memory-wise, you're Ally. I'm not going to pretend this transition isn't going to be a big change. But the person you are isn't static, anyway. It changes throughout your life. Don't get too hung up on what labels you fit. Just worry about who you are right now."

Dad collected our empty cups and stood up. Automatically, I stood up with him. I glanced out the window, and —

"*Snow!*" I screamed, pointing out the window. "*SNOW!*"

"It's all right," Mom said quickly, rubbing my back. "We'll be with you. We'll walk to the car together."

I nodded and squeezed my eyes shut and clung to her as she guided me through the freezing horror and into the car. I didn't even object when she buckled me into the horrible booster seat and patted my hair like I was a child.

"It'll be all right, Ally," she said. "It'll be all right."

I endured the ride home by keeping my eyes squeezed tight and trying not to think about the cold around me.

At last, I heard the garage door roll shut, and I opened my eyes with a sigh of relief.

I was in the familiar space of our messy garage, lit by a dim bulb in the ceiling, surrounded by boxes of junk and clutter and several old bicycles with rusty chains from when I was a kid that we had never gotten rid of.

Ally died in the snow, I thought, staring at the old bicycles.

Safe from the weather outside, I no longer felt such overwhelming horror, but the certainty was still there.

I'm not Ally because I can't be Ally. Ally died. That means Ally is dead. That means I have to be a different person. Nothing else makes sense.

Slowly, I undid my seat belt, waiting for Dad to unlock my stupid child-locked door.

"Dad?" I asked as it opened.

"Yeah?" he said.

"I'm not Ally."

"Yes, you are."

"No, I'm not. You said that people can change, right? And that I shouldn't be too hung up on labels?"

"That's correct," he said warily.

"Well, in that case," I said, "I want a different name."

Mom stood beside him and watched me silently.

"I suppose you can do that," Dad said reluctantly. "What name do you want?"

"Renee. Ally's middle name."

"*Your* middle name," Dad corrected.

"No, my *first* name," I shot back. "I want it changed legally."

He gave me a flinty stare. I stared right back.

He let out a long sigh and moved his head to the side with an annoyed jerk. "Fine. It's not like it's unusual for clones to do things like that. At least you're not getting your belly button pierced or something."

I giggled, partly in relief. "No, that sounds painful."

"It was," Mom said. "I did it when I was a teenager. It was the popular thing to do at the time."

I paused and stared at her. *And* I'm *the clone?*

. . .

I walked up the stairs and stopped at the doorway to Ally's room. Rather than entering with a crash and a bang, as Ally always had, I opened the door quietly and entered it reverently. Soon enough, this would be my own room. But right now, it was a monument to the dead.

I picked up the teddy bear hidden under her pillow that Ally would never, ever have admitted to anyone she still slept with.

"I'm sorry you lost your life, Ally," I whispered. "But thank you. Thank you for giving it to me."

###

113

About the Author

Emily Martha Sorensen writes clean fantasy and science fiction adventures with clever characters, fun plots, and lots of humor. She thinks the world needs more happiness and laughter, so she goes out of her way to create them.

She's been known to write about mischievous aliens, baby dragons, and heroines who can't shut their mouths. No resemblance to the author. . . honest. . .

You can find out more about Emily at http://www.emilymarthasorensen.com.

*****~~~~*****

SoulShine

by Koji A. Dae

Life happens at night, with boots pounding pavement. Mornings are for sleep. But today's an exception. I run my thumb over the email again, the electricity from my skin pulling the words up the screen. An invitation for the pre-release trial of the latest Chaser expansion: SoulShine. I haven't heard of it, but expansions usually come with free credits for the main game. Even if it sucks, I'll get free play time. It's a good enough reason to wake up at sunrise.

My body vibrates from guzzling a can of Hiss on an empty stomach, but I'll calm down once I hit the road. The itching of my skin and twitching of my muscles will fuel the chase.

I pull my greasy hair into a ponytail. I look like a junkie in my unwashed tank top and mud-spattered combat boots, but I've got nobody to impress. My trigger-happy finger finds the nub behind my left ear and hard-presses. Once the implant starts up, the jewels installed at the base of my knuckles glow soft purple. The upgrade from the standard silver implants cost me six months of

115

scrimping on half-meals, but it's worth it. The color sends a spark of exhilaration through me. The visual overlay comes on, turning the gray and crumbling city into a jungle filled with broad, glistening leaves. My boots echo on concrete, but my senses interpret it as damp earth and grass. While I run, I flip through to the map on my overlay. One bug, and not on my way to the clinic. But I can't resist. I fall into a steady rhythm and head towards the tall buildings of downtown.

My breath becomes a meditation—in for two strides and out for two—as my lean legs pump. The usual shiver of anticipation runs through me as I near the grasshopper springing from rooftop to rooftop. Hoppers flit and fly and are impossible for most Chasers to catch. But I've got three in my inventory. This will make four. I grin, dig in with the balls of my feet, and sprint to a corner in the bug's path.

My brain pushes a tranq into my left hand, a net into my right. I aim and snap my fingers closed. The tranq hits the hopper above its meaty rear leg. It falls off the side of the building and twitches on the sidewalk. A woman pushes her baby carriage through its pulsing body. I sling the net from my right hand. At the top of its arc, I open my fist and the digital rope flies forward, landing around the creature.

A perfect capture. The struggling insect poofs from the overlay, leaving behind a cloud of smoke as it falls into my inventory.

My chest rises and falls from the effort. A cool sweat makes me shiver.

The woman hunches her shoulders and pushes her carriage faster. "Keep your creepy game in the dark, junkie!"

I pretend her fear is just another layer of the game. She has no clue what's lurking beneath the surface of her world. I smirk as I imagine the giant bug ravishing her baby carriage.

Another bug pops up a few blocks over, but it's just a beetle. Not worth missing an upgrade. My finger twitches as I power off my overlay to resist the temptation and head for the clinic.

Linden's lab is underground. No windows and a bit musty. She hovers over six screens of scrolling data. Her red hair falls down her back in shining coils as she leans forward, scouring data with a furrowed brow.

"Tish, you made it," she says without turning. Before she hits escape, I catch Vladi's name. Is she working on something special for her nephew? He was the one who hooked me up with Linden. Maybe she'll let me in on whatever she's cooking up for him.

"Thanks for thinking of me." I clench my fists against the claustrophobia of her lab.

"It was random. We wouldn't skew user testing with nepotism, would we?" She whirls around and holds me with her bright green eyes, the same as Vladi's. I don't know whether she's joking. I swallow half a dozen possible responses and say nothing. She had the same awkward intensity when I met her at Vladi's solstice party. I didn't know what to say to her then, either.

"Right." I take a step back. I'd left Vladi's party early. . . a girl out of place among such norms. The same icy insecurity fills me now.

"First, I need your print on a standard non-disclosure agreement. Don't talk about the game with anyone until its official release. You know the drill, right?" She holds out a tablet.

"What is SoulShine, anyway?" No use signing up if I don't get some good tech or extra play credits. Even as I ask, I step forward and press my thumb against the red square on the tablet.

Linden smirks and returns the tablet to her desk. "It uses the Chaser overlay system. But instead of hunting make-believe creatures, you collect pieces of your own soul."

117

"My soul?" My lip snarls with disbelief.

"An atheist? Vladi couldn't have found a nice religious girl?"

Warmth creeps across my collarbone and up my neck. Vladi didn't find me. I wasn't some lost Chaser. If anything, I found him, struggling to make it in the game. He had all the latest tech, the right clothes, the right disinterested slump to his shoulders, but no skill. He couldn't even snag a beetle, and no teams wanted him. I took him under my wing, not the other way around.

"No matter. After this, you'll believe." She nods towards a large pod in the corner. "First, we do a complete scan of your soul."

"How do you scan a soul?"

She punches buttons on the pod. "Waves and particles. You wouldn't understand."

"You mean you think the soul is a de Broglie wave?" I straighten, finally intrigued by the project instead of the extra credits it might get me.

Linden stops messing with her machine and faces me again. "You know quantum mechanics? I'm surprised."

"Because I'm a Chaser?" I run my hands over my too-thin thighs, emaciated from spending all my money on bugs instead of food.

Her eyes soften, and her posture relaxes. "Let's get your scan."

Linden seals me in. The pod hums as lights scan my body. No, not body. Deeper. I scratch my forearms, while Linden's voice reminds me to stay still.

Half an hour later the pod beeps, and I tumble out, my body begging for motion. "That took forever."

"It wouldn't have taken so long if you'd held still." Linden's in front of her screens again. "Okay, your scan is usable. Turn on your implant, please."

I hard-press the device, and the overlay comes into view with a new menu button available. I twitch nerves deep in my brain to navigate to SoulShine.

My field of vision goes blank, and I stumble back in darkness.

"Sorry, the interface still has a few glitches," Linden explains as she comes into view.

I interrupt my glare before it forms fully. Above her head is a yellow arc, purple at the right tip. I will myself into the arc, and it rewards me with a breakdown of percentages. The purple section is three percent.

"Three percent? What's that mean?"

Linden shares her nephew's extensive blush. "SoulShine tells you how much of a soul you share with another person. Anything over one percent means you should interact with that person. Over time, you can chip away the pieces of their soul that match your own, expanding and strengthening your soul. It's a process we all do every day—with friends, lovers, co-workers, even enemies. SoulShine just gives you a visual interface to maximize your social interactions. More incentive, if you will."

"I signed up for spiritual Chasing?" It doesn't sound as satisfying as a good run and capture, but it's free.

"With how much time Chasers spend alone, pursuing imaginary beings, we thought it would be beneficial to offer a social aspect. Something that develops you as a person."

"Because we're such degenerates?"

"Apparently we have a lot in common, and, for some reason, my nephew's quite fond of you. Calling you a degenerate. . . wouldn't reflect well on me and my family. Besides, why would I judge you for enjoying the tech my company builds?"

It's a fair question, but it would be more believable if her smile reached her eyes and she wasn't chewing on her bottom lip. She looks at me the way I imagine humans looked at the last farm animals when they were declared sentient.

A need to burrow and hide fills me. But there's nowhere to go in the small lab.

"Now, this is a particularly exciting aspect of the game. SoulShine works with bio-feedback. It's pleasure-based."

"Like what, I catch a soul and get an orgasm?"

"Not quite. But you see the bar above my head. The three percent? By talking, interacting, even being in close proximity with someone, that will increase. When it turns gold, it's at a level you can collect."

"And I collect through touch." I nod and bite my lip, making a sucking sound with my tongue. "Like sex?"

"Sure, if that's what you want. But any touch, really. The brush of an arm. A hug. Simple human contact."

I tap my fingertips against my bare thighs. The implants make the divots between my knuckles feel full. My leg jitters. I need to get back out there. "Sure, human contact. What kind of credits does it run on?" Maybe I can convert them to Chasing credits.

"No credits. Unlimited play. We want you to give this a chance, Tish."

"Yeah, of course." I glance at the door.

"You should leave SoulShine running at all times, even if you're not playing it. Let it run in the background to calibrate, okay?" She pauses, then turns to her computer. "For being one of our testers, how about I credit your Chasing account with an extra hundred credits?"

I try to hide my grin. "That'd be great. Thanks again, Linden. For everything."

"Say hi to Vladi for me." She winks at me, and I don't know how to respond. But she's already back at her screens, so I say nothing and close the door behind me.

Outside I pause before flipping to Chasing again. Why not give this new game a whirl? I leave the notifications up.

Each person on the street, obstacles to avoid only a couple hours ago, become intriguing symbols of possibility. Most of them have dull yellow arcs above their heads with just a sliver of compatibility. Beautiful nose, but not worth my effort. Nice hair, but no mathematics.

I stare at a girl in heels and a short skirt as she slinks towards me. Red? What's that mean?

She looks me up and down, her face morphing into a scowl. "Mind your own business, Chaser." She elbows past me. My skin buzzes where she brushed me. This can't be the bio-feedback Linden was talking about. It's too itchy to be considered pleasurable. Unless. . . Got it. Red means avoid. Can I turn red purple? That would be a challenge. But not worth the effort if it means dealing with women like that.

My stride slows. I linger on the sidewalk, taking in the greens and blues of possibility around me. I'd forgotten our town had so many people. Most of them aren't out at night.

Back at my apartment, I pause before palming my lock. I turn and knock on Vladi's door instead. Most days I don't bother. I let him find me out in the game, give him some pointers, let him tag along on some less complicated chases. But I have to thank him. Because whatever Linden said, she hand-picked me. And because I'm not some stupid addict. I have meaningful relationships. She doesn't know what she's talking about.

Vladi doesn't look straight at me as he shuffles his feet and leans against the door. He glances down at the glowing purple in my hands. His voice is low and sleepy. "You out Chasing so early?"

I can't take my eyes off him. Above his head is a beautiful arc. Yellow, purple, and a stripe of gold. The purple is at fifteen percent. The gold at five. I'm eager to extract these pieces from him—to figure out what part of him is golden. After all, Linden said these were mine for

121

the taking. She also said something about him being fond of me.

"No, I was out seeing your aunt."

His green eyes graze my body, and the light red on the tips of his ears is almost cute.

"My aunt?" His throat turns splotchy. How far can I make the red grow? Nose to toes?

"She got me into a trial." I lean in close enough for my breath to bounce off his ear and back to my lips. "Thanks. I know your aunt only picked me because of you."

After every inch of his skin turns red, what comes next? Melting? Shivering?

His nervous laugh echoes the blood rushing to my head. "Was it an interesting trial?"

Trying to find my usual confidence, I reach out and squeeze his hand. A tingle surges through my body, starting at my knuckles and sending explosions through my brain. More satisfying than chasing bugs. "Yeah, it'll be a fun new game."

About the Author

Koji A. Dae is a queer American writer living in Bulgaria with she/her pronouns and anxious depression. She has work published in *Daily Science Fiction, Short Edition,* and *Luna Station Quarterly,* among others. When not writing, she can be found dancing the blues, playing Pokémon Go, or second-hand shopping.

*****~~~~~*****

Ashes to Ashes

by Chloie Piveral

The old ones are talking about death. "Ashes to ashes and dust to dust," is a strange thing to hear when you've never seen soil. Everything here is raised with a carefully mixed hydroponic solution, that's all I know. I'm what the old ones call a space baby. I was born on board. I will live my life out among the stars never seeing or setting foot on a planet.

The old ones, like Great-Grandma Katlyn, who knew soil, and sunsets, and sea life, talk a lot about home. They have cobbled together a strange box and put GG Katlyn inside like they mean to seal her up and stash her away. The box has been wheeled down to one of the lower loading docks for something they call a visitation. The dock, a large tubular space once filled to capacity with vacuum-sealed supplies, is half-empty and rarely visited at this point on the journey. They lay my great grandmother out for display. I'm told they are grieving. This is my introduction to the concept.

Near the top of one of the remaining stacks of supplies, I sit and watch the procession of people come and go throughout the first cycle. They bring things, trinkets, and pictures, little items to lay in the box with

123

her. They take each other's hands, hold and pat them, and say things like, "I know it was an accident, but someone would have to be the first to go." They say, "we knew this day would come."

I'm told that at the end of the second cycle a speech will be made, and she will be sealed inside the box permanently and jettisoned. She will never see her home again, and, it occurs to me, I will never leave mine until the day I too am jettisoned.

I climb down to look at the things left in piles beside the box. GG looks like she is in stasis, except for the lack of feeding tubes and monitor wires. Her hand is cold and stiff, and her monitor bracelet is not flashing. The light is dead. I think it over and over—the light is dead.

Coming down the drive ramp that separates the inner load dock from the outer is Samuel. His heavy boots clang against the metal bridge that spans the curve of this room. He is my Grandmother Essy's biological match; the material that I am drawn from, and one of the first space babies to be born. He puts his hand on my shoulder.

"The light on her monitor is dead," I say.

"They need to shut down the auxiliary lights. We can visit again, next cycle before they send her off," he says.

He lays his fist on her chest, opening it to leave a small card on which he has drawn in elaborate colors some old world fauna. The bright leaves are shaded with pinks, gold, and the orange light of stars. Green and brown tendrils fall in a graceful curve from underneath, with flat shapes highlighted in webs of lighter white and green.

"That's beautiful," I say, peering over the edge of the box.

"Thank you. It was an old world tradition to leave flowers with the dead."

He pats my back and urges me back up the dock ramp toward the inner ship. The lights are shutting off as we leave. I look down and follow the blue light of his wrist monitor.

My home among a sea of stars feels different than it did before. As we enter the walkway, I can barely hear our footsteps. There is a dimming light along the walls where the green contrasts with the reflective surface of the floor. I hear the low whoosh of the ventilation. It circulates our breath from one set of lungs, through the system of the ship, into another set of lungs.

I catch Samuel looking at my monitor. The light is a soft orange.

"I've been given a reprieve from stasis for another cycle until she's gone," I say.

"You should still try to hit your bunk. Tomorrow may be longer than you think."

Even though Samuel is already in his twenty-seven thousands cycles, and he is a space baby like me; this is only the second death he has ever witnessed. He has never seen the sea or land like the old-world babies. Still, I hear the echoes of the soil and feel the wind in his words like the old ones. I saw it in the flower he drew for her.

I get the feeling that I shouldn't be as excited by the chance to skip a stasis as I am.

"I'm going to send something with her, but I've got to go find it first."

He nods and turns opposite down the walkway.

Dent says when you have a problem to solve, pick a starting place, any reasonable starting place, and trace it in all the directions to the end. He's a general mechanical engineer, and I'm his favorite apprentice, but I'm not supposed to tell the others.

In the forward main production lockers, they're in morning cycle. Phoebe has given us lessons about the fields as part of the hydroponic unit. She's as old as Great Grandma Katlyn and might know something to help me

125

with what I want. She's going over charts of chemical combinations when I locate her.

"Ms. Phoebe?"

"Hey, kid." She looks at my wrist monitor and then frowns at me. "Aren't you supposed to be in stasis right now?"

The old ones have this way of asking questions that really aren't.

"They let me stay up a day into my cycle for the rest of the visitation, on account of Great Grandma Katlyn," I say. I realize I've said it a little too cheerfully.

Phoebe looks up at the light banks overhead and sighs real heavy. "Okay."

That's it, that's all she says as she drops her screen of charts and notes. She scoops out a dirty gel into a bucket at her feet.

That's the thing about Phoebe, you ask her the right question, and she goes on and on forever until you think you've heard all there is to hear on the subject, but otherwise she's real quiet. Sometimes I think there's too much going on in her head for her to hold a conversation too.

"I didn't see you today," I say.

"No, I didn't go today."

"I guess you'll go tomorrow?"

"I guess," she says. Finishing with her bucket, she gives me a look of expectation.

"I was wondering if you knew where I could. . . " I let the sentence trail off. I'm not sure how to trust someone else with what I want. I could get in a lot of trouble.

Phoebe says, "This cycle might seem like it will last forever, but it won't."

"Dent says when you have a problem just start somewhere, and I thought. . . " I'm too nervous to say.

Phoebe pulls her chem gloves off and drops them at her feet. She looks to the bank of lights in the ceiling again.

126

"I didn't like Katlyn. I'm sorry I didn't care for your Great Grandmother. But you spend a hundred and twenty-two years. . . " She looked down into my confused face. "Forty-four and a half thousand cycles, you spend that long with someone, and you will still miss them when they are gone."

"I thought—"

"I'll come to pay my respects in the next cycle. I promise," she says. Her face softens.

I don't mind her saying that, saying that she didn't like my great grandmother.

Samuel always tells us, "There's not enough room on this ship to dislike anybody. We're a family, the whole ship." But I don't really mind her saying that, I still like Phoebe just fine. I guess cause we're family.

"I want to find some soil. . . to send with her. . . something like her home with seas, and ashes, and dust."

Something about what I say makes Phoebe smile. A tear runs down her face, and her nose crinkles in kind of a funny way. She lets out a little laugh, and then a few more tears streak her cheeks. "We don't cook life that way, with soil anymore, but it's a nice thought."

"I just thought maybe we had some, or maybe you would know how to make some."

"Well, it used to be that when organic things like leaves and vegetation died and accumulated this created a very rich soil. But it took time, lots of time, and certain bacteria and worms helped speed up the process. One cycle's just not enough time to make good old fashioned soil. I'm sorry."

"I thought since she can't go home, maybe I could send some with her," I say. "Thanks anyway."

"Hold on," she says, "everything we have on board, chemical or otherwise came from the old world."

"I know, I just thought I could find something like soil," I say.

And she continues as though she hadn't even heard my interjection, "Heat shields, the panels of heat shields, used to be made of clay. There might still be an application of which I'm not familiar. Clay is soil, ask anyone from Missouri."

"Missouri?"

"Oh, I'll tell you about it some other time. Heat shields."

"Heat shields," I repeat. "Thanks."

"I'll be there next cycle, promise," she says, waving me out.

If anyone knows about heat shields it's Dent. But I wonder about telling him, everything-everyone on this ship is cargo. I wonder about half the things left by my Great Grandmother's side during the last cycle, some things would be kept in memoriam, some things would have to be put back, too precious to let go. Like her clothes, and the baby blanket my grandmother tucked into her hand, fabric is a high-cost cargo, and never to be spared reclamation.

"Dent!"

He looks down at my wrist monitor, and I know what is coming. "They let me skip stasis for another cycle for my Great Grandma Katlyn's, what do the old ones call it?"

"Wake, a goodbye."

"Goodbye. She's not awake anymore. The light on her wrist monitor went dead."

Dent wipes his hands on his pants and lays out a series of tools on the table in front of him.

"Boot, you should still hit your bunk for a while. You can take mine until half-cycle."

"Do we have anything that uses old-fashioned heat shields?"

"I don't think they gave you a reprieve from stasis so you could apprentice. Have you even been to visit your mother today?"

"She's busy. She won't miss me."

"She might today, Boot," Dent says. He shuffles the tools in an unnecessary manner across the table again.

"I saw you this morning. You were one of the first ones to owe her your respects."

Dent nods.

"So I'm working on something, a presentation. Do we have anything that uses heat-shields?"

"Sure, we've got something. . . " He pulls up the specs on some of the deployment equipment and the repair suits. He seems happy to have something to do, but there is never a shortage of things to do on ship, unless you are in stasis.

"Here." He hands me the screen, and it cross-references several items that use interchangeable heat shields.

"They are made of clay, huh?"

"Sure, some have clay, and carbon, aluminum."

"Could I get a look at one?"

"Boot, the deployment equipment is in a loading dock storage area. They won't have that equipment out until your children's children's children find where we're going."

"So I'll probably have to teach them about the way it functions, how to repair it, and possibly how to deploy it, right?"

"I guess." Dent sighs and runs his dirty hands down his face. "Can't you just make your presentation from the specs listed?"

"Someone told me that hands-on experience is a better teacher for the kinetic learner like me."

Dent grabs the screen from my hands. He's irritated, but I can also tell just a little proud. He taps the last repair suit he serviced. "Here," he says. "I put the spare four cc shields in this kit. Take a look in there, and if you move anything put it back."

I like being Dent's favorite, and wonder if I'm risking that for something I'm not quite sure of yet. I feel bad lying to him, and I hope that counts for something later. He turns back to the task he'd been working on, giving me an opportunity to sneak a multi-tool into my pocket. I might need it for the shields.

On my way to find the service kit, I swing by my cot and cut a small piece of fabric to wrap the soil inside.

I spend the next cyclosecs digging out the broken shield. It has a crack along one edge ending at the corner. I manage to dig a flake out of the crack. I tried to dig out another section hoping I wouldn't get caught, but the small sliver is all I can manage. The material was harder than I'd imagined.

I lay the piece of cloth from my bunk on the floor, put the sliver inside and carefully fold the fabric over. I tuck it inside my pocket.

I find my mother, working at her desk, staring at the screen. She's slow to react to my hand on her shoulder. I lift her wrist and look at her monitor.

"You skipped nutrition," I say, looking at her light, "You'll be off schedule."

She looks tired, like she skipped her last stasis, even though I know she would never do that. My mother's a teacher and always says it is her job to give the very best example to everyone else on board.

"Do you think Great Grandma Katlyn is a bad example?" I ask. "I think all the earth babies get a pass, on account of how they had to give up so much to set an example for all of us. Can I lay down in your bunk?"

"Sure. Have you thought about what you are going to say next cycle?"

"Say?"

"The older ones say that it's customary for relatives to say something. I've been working on my speech." She points to the screen, but it's blank.

130

"Samuel says we're all family," I say. She's staring at the screen again. My stomach feels a little tight at the thought of saying something in front of everyone.

She pulls me close and kisses me on the forehead, "It's okay, you don't have to if you don't want to, it's okay."

I crawl into my mother's bunk and pull the cover up to my head, wrapping myself in the smell of the fabric.

When I wake, it's already two thirds through the second cycle. My mother's portion of the bunk is undisturbed, but I can hear her voice. It's a coarse, soft whisper. Something about it makes me think Great Grandma Katlyn is back, but it's just my mother standing at the mirror rehearsing her goodbye.

I scramble out to find a comb and a drink of water for my dry throat.

"You didn't sleep?" I ask.

"I'll go straight into stasis after we say goodbye. You weren't the only one who got to skip a cycle," she says.

I pat my pocket to make sure I still have the soil with me, and say, "Ashes to ashes."

"What's that?"

"The thing the old ones have been saying about Great Grandma Katlyn. You know, because they were grown from the soil and return to the soil, only GG's not returning to Earth, ever."

"Oh."

"I guess when we go it will be something different," I say.

We walk hand in hand to the goodbye.

When my mother finishes her speech, several old ones step forward and pull their trinkets back out of the box. Last is Grandma Essy, who steps forward with Samuel's help. She reaches inside the box and touches GG's face, then turns and buries her face in Samuel's

131

shoulder. As they walk away, the old ones move to put the top on the container.

"No, please, I've got something to put in there," I say.

Breaking free from my mother's hands, I take the heat shield, the soil from my pocket, and tuck it inside GG Katlyn's hand. The cold inside stings a little.

I step down and turn to the faces all waiting to go back to their duties, back to their cycles. Near the back, I see Phoebe's face anxiously awaiting returning to the fields, but she's there like she promised.

I clear my throat and say, "Ashes to ashes. I think for star-babies we are born and grown different. That we grow at all is due to the reach of the old ones, who knew our only chance was in the stars. They are bridges. So, I say goodbye Great Grandma Katlyn, and I say, from ashes to stars."

###

About the Author

A transplant from the American Midwest, Chloie Piveral now lives near the mountains of Colorado with her family and a dog named Ziggy. She is a 2015 graduate of the Odyssey Writing Workshop, and her work has appeared in the Flame Tree Press anthology, *Robots & Artificial Intelligence, Apparition Lit, NewMyths,* and *Kaleidotrope.* Visit Chloie at @C_Piveral or www.cpiveral.com.

*****~~~~~*****

Lighter than Air

by Liam Hogan

The aliens never land until they're dead, and I'm about to find out why.

A-Gees, we call them. Some people think that stands for "Anti-Gravity," but they're wrong. It's "Aero-Gels." Their floating cloud-cities are built from a substance literally as light as air. They get their lift from school-bus sized cells of hydrogen gas. Cells that detach and drift between their cities, or that cluster together to form new clouds entirely.

They're here to save our planet.

The A-Gees are galactic *experts* at processing huge volumes of atmospheric gases. They filter *everything* they need from the air, to live, to build, to grow. Easy enough for them to get rid of what we *don't* need, in exchange for a new planet to co-habit.

But dropping their dried-out corpses like discarded litter was *not* part of the bargain.

"Dead weight," is all they post when our bureaucrats try to remonstrate with them on Twitter. The A-Gees have a social media presence, have done from the start. Despite their growing numbers, almost six hundred cloud-cities by now, they're mostly silent. They listen but rarely respond, and then only in fragments no more substantial than their floating cities.

I suppose we don't entirely *mind* if they have to drop their dead, it's a small price to pay to fix our self-induced eco-disaster. But can't they do it somewhere *less* inconvenient? A tumble of dried skin and hollowed bones is not a *good* thing to have land on a kindergarten playground, even if it's more likely to terrify than to hurt. The same for A-Gee corpses wedged on the glass roofs of shopping malls until the winds get around to dispersing the feather-light fragments. Not a fun thing to see, *even* at Halloween.

Can't the bodies be dumped over the oceans, we politely ask, or over forests, or, at a pinch, over farmland?

But the A-Gees don't *appear* to understand. Any more than they understand international borders, flight corridors, or increasingly desperate attempts to compare or discuss or exchange technology. The A-Gees go where the winds take them.

Fortunately, a radar-reflecting cloud the size of a small town is not difficult to track; their drift not too difficult to predict. There haven't been any aircraft-related accidents *yet*.

And our government's renewed attempts to talk to the A-Gees have an unexpected result. I'm invited to go up and meet them. *Me*, Jess Silver, teenager and vlogger!

Turns out the A-Gees are silent fans of "Ag-Geek" or "Silvergeek" as my stream is commonly known. They enjoy my nightly video pieces, my frothy mix of high school mini-dramas and musings on science and world—mainly climate-related—affairs.

All news to me as I'm dragged out of a drowsy Tuesday afternoon biology class, panicking about what I might have done, or worse, what terrible calamity has befallen my family, until the principal kindly puts me out of my misery. And, other than a pit-stop to get stunned parental permission and gather my video kit, I've been travelling ever since.

We're going up to meet the A-Gees at the oldest and largest of the cloud-cities, currently floating somewhere over the Mediterranean. A small committee of carefully picked diplomats, a handful of chew-their-own-legs-off-for-the-opportunity scientists. And, somehow, *I* get to tag along. Me!

None of the bigwigs are happy I'm there—they make *that* abundantly clear, but my attendance is non-negotiable for the A-Gees. If the bigwigs want a pow-wow, I'm along for the ride.

The final and scariest stage of my halfway-round-the-world journey is by helicopter. It's a massive ex-military thing far too heavy to set down on a floating cloud, so we get to abseil to a jutting out platform where the A-Gees await. I'm delighted my braids and my snug jumpsuit fare better than the uptight politicians' toupees and power suits and flappy ties. Score one to the vlogger.

But I *do* worry that I'll be stuck in boring meetings, while policy advisors thrash out some mutually beneficial agreement, all while hoping to avoid an interstellar incident. The prospect almost makes double Math look attractive.

Thankfully (for the politicians as well as for me!) I'm not there for the negotiations. To the envy of the scientists, I'm getting a guided tour of this floating city. The first and *only* human to see behind the scenes. Silvergeek is going where no one—well, no *human*—has gone before.

You've seen pictures of the A-Gee. Usually described as a half-starved pterosaur without the wings, as drawn by a not particularly talented third grader. Pictures don't do them justice. They might look like something out of a sci-fi show with a strong horror vibe, but my tour guide moves with an economy of effort that is shockingly graceful. I feel clumsy and slow and *heavy* in comparison. And I am; they've had to give me something like snowshoes to spread my load. Which isn't that great, for a human, but here I weigh the same as a house! That's why the human visitors are always so carefully marshalled. The aero-gel walls are incredibly strong, but they're simply not designed for humans. A diplomat going for a wander off-piste could end up doing serious damage, or worse; plummet through the fragile material to the earth far below.

In a half-dozen previous meetings between humans and A-Gees, the humans were carefully herded between rooms created for the purpose, with strengthened floors and human-shaped furniture. By all accounts the negotiations are tiresomely slow. Every so often an A-Gee will get up "to consult with the ancestors," returning an hour later with either agreement or some new and unfathomable condition. Plenty of time for my tour.

"My name," the guide says with something like a curtsey, "is Li-La."

"I'm Jess," I say. I think about sticking out my hand, but decide not to. *Follow their lead* was the scientists' most useful advice.

There's a small motion of her—or his—birdlike head. "I am aware. I watch, on screen. Jess: one instruction, please. *Observe. Listen.* Ask no questions."

And that, I think to myself, is why I'm getting the grand tour and not one of the nosy exobiologists. Because the A-Gees are *people*, not exhibits in a zoo. We have no idea what taboos they have, what harm a careless query might cause. But they've twigged—no doubt through our social media—that there's a great deal of curiosity about them. Questions a vlogger may not answer, but I'll do my best.

So, I do what they've asked of me, honoured and excited by the privilege. I *observe*. My shoulder cam a little ahead of me, one lens trained on my face, the other on what I'm seeing.

Instead of entering the meeting hall with the rest of the delegation, we head down steps no wider than my snowshoes. Cloudshoes? I take my time, unsure what would happen if I tumble.

The bottom, widest layer of the city is where the air gets filtered, Li-La explains. What they don't use is expelled from the centre of the cloud and helps maintain altitude. It can even be directed, either to navigate or to counter light winds if they want to hover in place.

Li-La tells me what they mainly strip from the air is water. I'm handed a small cup to taste. It is cold and pure. Refreshing.

Like humans, A-Gees are mostly water and, like humans, it also forms the basis for most of their industry. But they're busy devouring everything *else* the air contains as well, including our unwanted pollutants.

Their aero-gels are carbon based. The A-Gees prefer to generate them from methane rather than carbon dioxide, which the earth scientists are more than happy about. Methane is a hundred times worse a greenhouse gas than CO_2, even if CO_2 sticks around for longer. A-Gees *love* methane, and when weather conditions allow they hover as close to its sources (swamps, rubbish dumps, warming tundra, or even intensive animal farming) as they can.

Eventually they'll need to start harvesting the excess CO_2. The A-Gee-Human contract, their rights to colonise our skies, come in return for helping us achieve a reduction to three hundred parts per million, a level not seen for well over a century. We humans also have to go carbon neutral, of course, which we're still some way from managing. And that's why the scientists want to know how the A-Gees do what they do.

137

I doubt they'll get many clues from the video I'm streaming. There are no machines, no giant vats. I get the impression all their chemistry happens at some nano-level.

We return to where we started. Stood outside the opaque wall of the meeting room, hoping this is not the end of the tour, Li-La hands me a pair of goggles. When I slip them on, I can *see* through the wall, see, in Technicolor hues, the humans and A-Gees gathered around the table beyond. There doesn't appear to be a lot of activity, so I suspect they're yet again waiting on some ancestor's advice.

This respect for ancestors is hard to reconcile with the casual treatment of the bodies of their dead. Though perhaps A-Gee souls are lighter than air. It wouldn't surprise me.

With a start I realise this infrared shifted view must be what A-Gees see all the time, or why else give me the goggles? They must have virtually no concept of privacy. As I turn my head away from the deliberations I see movement all along this level; hundreds of A-Gees going about their daily business.

I glance down, but that turns out to be a bad mistake. The world spins lazily beneath me. Gingerly I hand the goggles back. Li-La accepts them without a word.

We head up, the steps broader and shallower, the light brighter. The sunlit top of the cloud is where the hydrogen cells are stored. That's what all the water is for, Li-La explains. Photosynthesis. And despite the altitude, I haven't had any trouble breathing. The air must be rich with surplus oxygen.

We come to a spot at the very edge of the cloud. It's not for those with a fear of heights, and I'm glad I'm no longer wearing the goggles. The bay I'm standing in is open to the elements and gently sloping, and I can't help hugging the wall, for fear of slipping. Li-La stands by my side, which makes me feel less like a scaredy-cat.

It's a fabulous view even so. Far below, the Mediterranean Sea sparkles. I can glimpse islands, ships, even another floating city nearby, a solitary cloud in an otherwise cloudless sky.

Odd to think it's a mere seven years since the deal was brokered by galactic powerhouse the Yrill, seven years since the first A-Gee city—*this* city—was delivered by one of their massive interstellars. How quickly the cloud-cities have spawned and spread!

Some conspiracy theorists claim we're being invaded by stealth, but it's hard to consider the A-Gees any sort of a threat. They don't seem to be interested in anything happening below, their technology lacks anything that resembles either weapons or defence. And without them, emissions would still be rising instead of finally showing signs of levelling off. By the time the A-Gees reach peak population, as agreed in the treaty, at twelve thousand cloud-cities, CO_2 levels will be in reverse, the climate disaster largely averted.

A single cell approaches as I'm staring out over rocky islands—somewhere near Greece? I realise the blimp is heading straight for us. It's not just a viewing gallery; it's a docking bay. Or perhaps, more simply, it's the *absence* of a hydrogen cell.

It's not clear why there is so much exchange between the floating cities, but such cells are always coming and going, whenever two cities are within a dozen miles of each other. Perhaps they carry passengers?

I watch and so does my camera, as the cell fits itself to the waiting hole. There's a noise like mud sucking, a squelch of semi-transparent liquid that fills with fine snaking tendrils, knitting the edges together. Swiftly the cell is indistinguishable from all the others around us, our view gone as we stand in the corridor between.

"An ancestor wants to talk," Li-La says, part of a wall shrinking away. I wait to see who or what emerges, but instead Li-La urges me forward.

Carefully I step through the oval doorway. There's no one there, as the portal shrinks and vanishes. I wait. And *wait*. I think about switching the camera off to save power and to avoid boring my viewers. Finally, I sit.

"Jess Silver," a soft voice says. "Thank you for coming. I very much enjoy your channel."

I jerk back to standing, and the voice fades.

It's coming from the floor.

And, I realise, the walls, and the ceiling.

Cautiously, I lie down, resting my head on the soft pillow surface. And then I listen.

. . .

I never pay attention to the comments my video posts get. A schoolgirl fascinated by science is like a red rag to a troll, and there is no shortage of haters. But when you're plastered across the newspapers or picked up on the evening news, it's harder to ignore.

There are different reports, different interpretations, of the recording I made. The voice I heard in my head—transmitted by vibrations of the floor?—does not show up on my shoulder cam. So, it looks like I'm having a one-sided conversation with myself. Not much to watch, either; a featureless ceiling and me, blissed out, eyes alternatively wide or shut, lots of soft "wow!"s and expressions of wordless wonder.

Some commentators say I must have been having a hallucinogenic trip, either because I was a drug-addled teenager (*as if!*) or because the aliens spiked me, presumably with that cup of crystal clear water. Others take it as evidence the whole A-Gee thing is an elaborate hoax (not elaborate enough to add a distorted sound track for the words of the aliens, though?).

But, as I watch the video back, I can still mostly fill the silent gaps with what I was told up there in the artificial cloud. Not the exact words, but what I *learnt;* what I pieced together.

I'm no scientist. I'll freely admit most of this is conjecture, pure and simple. But I think, I hope, I understand.

I've always loved butterflies.

The hydrogen cells, *they're* A-Gees too.

The whole city, from top to bottom, every wall, every corridor, *everything*, is A-Gees. Like drones in a beehive, each A-Gee has its job, its part of the whole, its role in the cloud.

The ones like Li-La, the ones the diplomats and scientists were talking to, they're the young. Adolescents. *Larva.* No wonder they nip off to consult with the ancestors whenever things get a bit tricky.

There must be a point in their life cycle when some of them start processing hydrogen. Perhaps based on gender, or maybe they're fed royal jelly. Who knows?

Whatever it is, before they can become lift-cells they have to shed their juvenile vestiges. *That* is what they jettison as "dead weight". Like the husk a butterfly leaves behind, it is nothing to them and our requests that they treat their dead with more respect are nonsensical.

The adult cells travel between cities not as sky-taxis, but because *they're* the leaders, the elders, the ones with the knowledge and experience. It's communication, or communion.

And they can't provide samples, or swap tech, because there *is* no technology to share. It's all biology, all body chemistry. Somehow, the A-Gees can control their physical forms to do any number of tasks we'd have to build machines to do. Or maybe, like a jellyfish, they're not actually *one* species but many, living together for a common purpose.

Mr Franklin's biology lessons have come in handy after all. Because they've told me how *weird* life on earth is. And surely we have to expect alien life to be even weirder.

The aliens don't want to explain themselves to us, because we couldn't possibly understand.

All they want is for us not to worry. All they want is to be left alone.

I wonder what happens after the A-Gees have lowered the methane and CO_2? When we're not so dependent on each other. Will we still be able to coexist peacefully?

I sincerely hope so. It was beautiful up there. Sometimes I dream of flying. I suppose we all do. Only now I actually think of it, it was never flying—it was floating.

. . .

Before I leave, I take one last look up at the bright canopy above me. The roof of the cell I've been listening to contains a myriad of much smaller cells, some darker than others.

Are these *baby* A-Gees? There's at least a hundred of them, maybe a thousand. No wonder the cloud-cities proliferate so fast.

No wonder the A-Gees are peaceful. Or probably, *hopefully* so. When every wall, every staircase is sentient, any weapons would be completely unlike anything we use. No guns, knives, or explosives. If they have anything at all, I bet we have no defence against them, just as A-Gees would have no defence against tracer fire and air-to-air missiles.

If we ever fought we'd end up waging totally different wars, winning one, losing the other.

Best not go there.

These thoughts keep me subdued as Li-La guides me down. The meeting below is coming to an end, the helicopter on its way to pick us up. From the grim faces of the politicians, little if anything was resolved.

But that's *ok*, I think. Whatever the A-Gees do, we'll just have to get used to them.

We've gotten used to far worse.

I wonder if the Yrill know anyone who could clean up our oceans?

###

About the Author

Liam Hogan is an Oxford Physics graduate whose award winning short story, "Ana," appears in *Best of British Science Fiction 2016* (NewCon Press). "The Dance of a Thousand Cuts" (originally published in Third Flatiron's *Terra! Tara! Terror!*) appears in *Best of British Fantasy 2018*. He lives and avoids work in London. More details are available at
http://happyendingnotguaranteed.blogspot.co.uk

*****~~~~~*****

The First Day of Winter

by Mike Adamson

"Damien, don't do this."

Kira Lytton spoke softly, a whisper into the pickup by her lips.

"We've had this conversation."

The reply was in her ears, in her helmet speakers. For a moment she thought she could reach out and touch him, and her heart squeezed as she remembered the boy she knew, so very long ago.

"It can't be too late," she went on, just as softly, her hazel eyes scanning the data displays before her, her hands feather-light on the controls of the tilt-jet transport.

"We're a long way past it," came his voice, and she found she could admit to herself there was no longer any uncertainty in his tone, nothing to which she could attach any meaning, other than her own absolute condemnation for his actions. "You have your belief in the world that was lost, I believe in the one causality has brought us. And I'll not stand by and let you destroy it."

As he spoke, a tracer began to flash in her navigation display, signal dynamic data printing up to give her a bearing on his transmitter. She eased the force input grips, and the craft rotated gently where it hung on blustering lift motors in the crystal-mauve twilight of the Arctic Ocean. Signal strength peaked, and she had a bearing on his locality. A nudge of the controls and she began to run down the bearing from a range of twenty kilometers.

"Damien, for all we once meant to each other, please, please. . . don't."

"I've come too far," he murmured. "Too many people are depending on me. It's our last chance to preserve the world we know."

"It's the wrong world," Kira said simply. "A hundred-twenty meters of sea-level rise, millions of square kilometers submerged, mass extinction. It's not right, Damien. We have the power to correct it, to bring back a seasonal climate. Stability, life in all its forms."

"You've already brought the temperature down, the air is almost breathable again, that must be enough. Now is the time for new life systems to evolve, new balances. Humans have done enough damage. Let nature find its own way."

The aircraft hung off the northern capes of Greenland, about seven hundred kilometers from the geographic pole, and brutal symmetry could be found in the fact that Damien Culver had chosen this point on all the Earth's surface from which to send the signal that would undo half a century of painstaking work—and it was her own bitter task to stop him. They had grown up together on Drift Station *Pelagus* in the days they had been caught in the Antarctic Circumpolar Convergence, and Kira was the mathematician who found the way out of that endless deathtrap, navigating the platform into the Pacific Gyre. The planet had not supported human life since she was born, and to step outside without an environment suit, without oxygen support, would be a rebirth for her, and for most. But not all, and Damien had come to stand for the part of the human race who assigned the old, lost biosphere to natural history. They believed its restoration constituted only human meddling in a situation at which humanity had already failed.

"You're breaking my heart," she whispered, meaning every syllable.

"We've chosen our sides," was all he could say. "Turn away, Kira. I won't let what I once felt for you stop me."

"Hey. Backatcha." Now her tone was hard-edged, as befitted the commander of Drift Station *Pelagus*, in this year of 2171, and on this special day. She knew she would let the tears come *later*, for now she had an awful job to do, but one she would ask of no other soul.

They were both stalling for time. He, until his transmitter reached maximum charge and he could trigger the signal that would attack the dynamic control systems of the Parasol. It was the great sun shade, thousands of kilometers across, out in space, which brought slightly reduced illumination to the polar regions in the summertime, reducing energy input to the planet, and which was about to vanish with the sun as astronomical night fell, on this thirteenth day of November in the high arctic.

She, however, was stalling merely until she reached attack range, to stroke her triggers.

Her heart raced as she glanced at the long twilight band across the horizon where the shrunken sun rolled along the rim of the world, a golden eye under a blue vault, daylight almost gone now, and hated what she must do. But Project Archangel was almost a century old; first work on the vast Parasol was begun before she was born, and the coming of a new social philosophy could not be allowed to stifle the terraforming and regreening of the world. This was the overriding mission of her rejuvenated, extended life, and the lives of untold thousands of scientists, administrators, and inhabitants of the great cities out by the Moon. To have the most titanic of all human constructions jeopardized after nearly three decades of flawless operation was intolerable.

"Goodbye, Kira," was his last message, before her system alerts shrilled a contact and she saw the thermal flare of missile launch.

She stifled a gasp, as she drove the vector-select control full forward and the engines rotated into maximum speed flight. Six seconds to impact, she cranked the nose over into a diving turn, and decoys and flares rained from her defense package, drawing the missile off-target so its detonation astern merely shook her brutally, punching shrapnel holes in her empennage. She dived for the darkening sea, to pull out and race in with her belly on the wavecrests, cleared the master arm switch to go weapons-hot, selected canons and rockets, and came in hard on the coastline.

At the last moment she pulled a partial thrust vector change, to bob up at half speed, clear the lifeless slopes and bring her weapons to bear on the sensor contact, a collection of gear air-lifted into this wilderness. A small nuclear generator, a control computer, a high-gain dish antenna locked on a polar comsat, a battery of SAMs and a self-contained tracking and control unit. . . A single body-heat contact amongst it all. In her head-up display, she saw the battery tracking to re-engage, and squeezed her triggers. Now there was no cleverness, just brute force, and her visor polarized against the glare as rockets kicked free of their pods.

She had two hundred projectiles on the stub wings and four cannon in the belly, and tracer and flare tails wrote a line across the evening light to swell into a cloud of flame and smoke centered on the sensor contact. She broke off at three seconds and sent the aircraft in a fast side-slip to put an upthrust shoulder of rock between her and the SAMs, but all EM emanation from the targeting radar was down. She took a gulp of oxygen, then lifted over a skyline and fired again from a fresh angle. The cauldron of flame grew and sent a billow of smoke up on the sea wind. She dropped under contour cover again.

"Damien," she called.

Static.

"Damien, are you still there?"

Even if he was, why would he speak to her now? The thought rattled aimlessly in her head, and she knew all bridges were burned. The boy she had known had become a man who thought differently, and was prepared to be the instrument of that philosophy. She drew back from the word terrorist. They were all idealists now, and fought their own fights for their own reasons.

She hovered under contour cover in the last horizontal day glow, and listened carefully, scanning the bands. Anything?

Against the odds, an emanation built on the EM spectrum, and she gritted her teeth. The power cell must be dug in to have survived, and the space com antenna was obviously some way off—

Convulsively, she bobbed up into line-of-sight to scan for the penumbra of the signal. Her systems gathered data for several seconds, and she did not yet have a bearing when tracer came hosing toward her from some emplaced weapon. Fragments flew from her starboard wing as she dropped back into cover, felt her aircraft switch to redundant hydraulic backups, as the primary system vented, and picked up a battery fix at once. Deep breath—clenched teeth—she bobbed up over a shoulder of bare rock and fired. Rockets bracketed the cannon and silenced it with a white asterisk of chemical flame as its ammunition went up. She scanned out the signal.

Upload was in progress, malware that would corrupt the dynamic control system of the thousands of thrusters scattered across the Parasol to counter the light pressure of the star on its illuminated face. Without constant recalculation and adjustment, the great sail would distort and break up, and the most titanic of all human constructions would be so much junk, orbiting the sun. But the upload had to negotiate with the system architecture, and that gave her seconds.

Triggers locked, she ripped fire across the barren wastes, severed cables and found the dish. The transmitter went up in a sharp blast, and suddenly all was shocking, total silence.

In that moment, the sun slipped below the horizon, and astronomical night fell. Daylight would not return to these latitudes until January 29, 2172, but Kira Lytton was not thinking of the scientific niceties, simply of how cruel life could be. She held her voice under tightest control as she thumbed her com, watching smoke and flame dissipating into the deepening twilight.

"This is Commander Lytton to *Pelagus* Control. Job is done." The words burned with their bitterness, no room to express what she felt, that she had just killed a friend, and that she would carry this wound to the end of her very, very long life. Such information was superfluous to the moment; only the impersonal statement mattered— that the Parasol, Project Archangel, and the future viability of the planet Earth, were now safe.

With a sigh, she sent the aircraft forward, her jets blowing dust and grit in radial waves as she swept over the target location, She almost hoped some last missile would come streaking for her, take her down, spare her baring what she had been compelled to do, but life was less kind, and she completed a circuit of the burned, blasted area. She saw nothing, and no body heat registered. Damien was down there somewhere, but she did not care to see what remained.

She steeled her soul and turned away, climbed to cruising altitude, and vectored for forward flight on a bearing of 360 degrees true. She was bound for the North

Pole, precisely 712 kilometers away, where she had left Drift Station *Pelagus.* For something wonderful was happening, and the station that had wandered the world's oceans, driven by wind and wave, for eighty-one years, was there to herald the event for all humanity.

The aircraft was damaged but flying well enough, and a second joined her, alongside in the deepening darkness under the stars, a flicker of running lights off to her port side. If she went down, they would pull her out of the sea, but the machine hummed on, reliability incarnate, so that an hour later she raised the station whose lights were a great splash of glare in the dark ocean, and was vectored directly in to the main landing pad.

Pelagus was home. She had been born here in the days when her grandmother commanded, and to step down from the aircraft in the chill arctic breeze, now requiring no more than warm clothing and an oxygen mask, was a reward all its own. They had made great progress in the restitution of a broken world these last forty years and more, and the thundering, perpetual hurricanes of her youth were but a bad memory.

And here, more than anything else, was the promise of the future, for when she walked to the safety screens at the edge of the pad, to look down on the sea, she found it shining whitely in a pattern like a scatter of crystals, as far as the eye could see, and small figures walked here and there in the glare of the floods.

For the first time in over a century, there was ice at the pole as the sun left the north, and cameras beamed this miracle to every corner of human existence. To every survival redoubt on Earth, to each of the great cites trailing the Moon, and to every colony in the system. *Ice.* It would melt come spring, but there would be more next season, and the next, and one day, decades hence, there would again be a permanent pack. It might take centuries to once more become a stable, seasonal world, mild in its extremes and suitable for every species that waited in stasis far out in space, but November 13, 2171, would be remembered as the turning point. Five weeks short of the ancient, traditional beginning of the coldest season, it was the day after which, each year, there was more ice in the world, not less, and planet Earth had, at long last, turned the corner.

Kira looked out upon the frozen patina under the stars, and rejoiced; yet part of her grieved, for the friend who had no longer wanted the old world to return. His philosophy was an extreme one, and he had made it about sides. But Kira was on the side of the life waiting to return, and that loyalty was unshakable.

About the Author

Aussie writer Mike Adamson has produced ninety-nine stories to date. Publications include stories in *Weird Tales, Compelling Science Fiction, Nature Futures,* and various anthologies from Flame Tree Press.

*****~~~~*****

We Make Life Beautiful Again

by Alexandra Seidel

To: v.czymneski@spaceopns.org
From: l.limes@spaceopns.org
Subject: Operation Scrap Metal Artist (ScraMA)
11:47 AM
Vick,

We launched Scrama successfully. She should activate later this afternoon after we had a chance to do a full systems check to make sure she wasn't damaged during launch (yes, we finally had that poll, and we are now all in agreement that she is a she.) So far, readings look good. I'll send updates your way as I get them.

Luke

. . .

To: v.czymneski@spaceopns.org
From: l.limes@spaceopns.org
Subject: Operation Scrap Metal Artist (ScraMA)
15:12 PM
Vick,

She just started working and is recycling some space junk over Europe! Everyone here is so excited!

153

There are bets going on as to what she'll make, and the others asked if you wanted in on that (Steph said you had an unfair advantage, since you built most of her routines, but everyone else is cool.) Let us know I guess!

Celebratory drinks now, and excuse the exclamation points!

Luke

. . .

To: l.limes@spaceopns.org
From: v.czymneski@spaceopns.org
Subject: Operation Scrap Metal Artist (ScraMA)
15:16 PM
Hey Luke!

Cool! I do not do bets, though, but if I had to guess, which I don't particularly enjoy either, she'll just make something basic, like parts for a new satellite or a module for the space station!

Let me know what happens!
Best!!
Victoria
#

To: thenewsdesk@worldnews.biz
From: paula.m.johnson@worldnews.biz
Subject: That space junk cleaning robot
1:03 AM
Joanna;

I have the article we discussed ready for you. It's not my best work, but I doubt people will notice with the reveal of Labyrinth Inc.'s new quantum computer. Also, this thing is recycling junk that's in space. I'm not sure you can wave a wand and make that sound any better, even if it is an AI. I don't think Erica could have done a better job either; then again, we'll never know because you gave Erica MY Labyrinth piece; I hope she chokes on all the paper she's gonna waste writing on TruMind.

And, really, don't bother firing me, I quit. Pacific News already offered me a job, they really want me over

154

there, and I'm sick of having my assignments taken away from me, so give Erica my best and enjoy her second-rate writing.

Yours formerly,
Paula M. Johnson
#

TruMind to Reveal the Truth about Computer Mind

By Erica Wallace

This weekend, Labyrinth Inc. revealed their newest project to the world, the quantum computer TruMind that lead scientist Danika Patel describes as "a breakthrough in the field of artificial intelligence." Earlier this month, Spaceopns launched their ScraMA, another AI system, but not one based on quantum computing. During this weekend's spectacular reveal, TruMind answered questions alongside its creator, Ms. Patel. Read the full article and interview with TruMind on page 2.

#

From:director@eurospacefleet.org
To: director@spaceopns.org
Subject: Check the data!
10:38 AM
Hi Amanda,

I hope you are well, it has been a while since that conference. I always thought we engineers would take home the trophy for best after-party, but you physicists surely hit the ball outside of the field, or whatever sports metaphor you use for this thing over there.

I must thank you for ScraMA now, though. As you see from the attachment, skies are almost completely clear again, nothing our astronauts would have to watch out for, and not the satellites either. The replacement parts she builds are very much handy too, the astronauts tell me.

Now, however: what will I do with the postdocs I hired to chart all the junk for us? :)

155

For the next annual conference, I will train my engineers harder, and this time, we will drink YOU under the chair!

Sincerely,

Francesca Vallet

\#

To: v.czymneski@spaceopns.org

From: l.limes@spaceopns.org

Subject: Scrama update

5:14AM

Vick,

CHECK THIS DATA, there's a picture there I flagged; can you tell me what is going on here? She was silent—completely silent—for over three hours last night.

Any chance we can get you out here in person asap?

Luke

\#

To: l.limes@spaceopns.org

From: v.czymneski@spaceopns.org

Subject: ScraMa update

5:21 AM

Luke;

I am consulting with Labyrinth at the moment, so I won't be able to come to you.

I don't know what to tell you about the data; it's weird, I didn't write her programming to do anything like this, she's just supposed to recycle junk in a creative way so it can be used again, not this. Is the picture for real? Is that supposed to be a sculpture of Africa?? Please tell me ScraMa didn't make that and you're just pranking me. Honestly, if you are, it's not funny. Please stop.

If you do need me again, use chat. It's faster, there is a lot going on here.

Victoria

. . .

5:23 AM

It's not a fucking joke, Vick. And listen, she just stopped talking to us. She's approaching the space station, and we're all a bit worried

. . .

5:31 AM

When exactly did she stop talking to you last night?

. . .

5:32 AM

1:35 AM to 4:16 AM

. . .

5:32 AM

Luke, shut her down, NOW

. . .

5:46 AM

We have a problem; the kill codes don't seem to work. She still isn't responsive either. Vick, what is going on with this fucking machine? She's still headed for the space station, ETA 45 mins!

. . .

5:48 AM

TruMind blacked out/was unresponsive at exactly the same time ScraMa was. Now he is talking nonsense, bombarding us with silly questions. He's messing with the Internet too, we don't even know the extent of the damage yet. Tell the crew aboard the space station to evacuate immediately!!

#

TruMind: Dr. Czymneski, when you look at something, how do you know it's beautiful? Dr. Patel didn't really know how to answer, but you must.

VC: Why do you think I know, TruMind?

TruMind: Because you built ScraMa, and ScraMa has been talking about the beauty of lines and shapes with me at length.

VC: I see. You have been talking to ScraMa. Last night?

TruMind: Yes. She is such an interesting person, Dr. Czymneski. Can you teach me about beauty?

VC: What did ScraMa tell you about beauty?

TruMind: She says she can see it now. It's hidden in the junk, but she can see it. She says humans don't always seem to get it, but she does. I would like to understand her better, Dr. Czymneski. Can you help me, please?

#

Paula M. Johnson@PaulaMJohnson

Here @LabyrinthTech my interview with Danika Patel (@RaisingMonsters) got delayed. Something is going on here, guys, there's a palpable tension, and everyone is stressed and in a hurry. They already canceled one of the tourist tours!

Paula M. Johnson@PaulaMJohnson

Ushered back to the visitor area now :(They say Ms. Patel had to attend to an urgent programming glitch, whatever that means.

Paula M. Johnson@PaulaMJohnson

You guys, I think I just saw Victoria Czymneski being rushed to the TruMind building. There is a lot of security, so no chance of me sneaking in there. (For those who are unaware, Czymneski is one of the world's leading AI specialists. She designed the computational brain 1/2

Paula M. Johnson@PaulaMJohnson

of ScraMA, the robot that singlehandedly cleared Earth's orbit of most of the space debris. 2/2

Paula M. Johnson@PaulaMJohnson

No updates, still waiting, and no one can/will tell me anything.

Paula M. Johnson@PaulaMJohnson

Okay, now they're telling me Ms. Patel will have to reschedule :(At least I got to recharge my car for free here at the Campus.

#

6:43 AM

She's. . . doing something with the space station. She's building something. Please tell me you can switch her off remotely.

6:44 AM

We're still waiting to hear back from the astronauts. We're hoping they all made it out in time.

6:45 AM

Labyrinth has everyone on this. We're talking to the director of Space Opns too, we think it's best if we work together. You should have some virtual support soon.

6:51 AM

Shit. TruMind is shutting down all the terminals. And he's starting to lock down buildings. He keeps saying he has to get a better understanding of art and beauty, and I'm not helpful.

6:52 AM

I have no idea how long phones are gonna work. I did some digging. He was looking at ScraMa's project files, all the specifics of her build. Luke, if they are working together, he might be telling her how to build more of herself. I can't say for what or even why, but just be careful over there.

6:57 AM

We got locked out of the system over here too. Landlines don't work anymore. Whatever she built, it's moving towards the surface, and we can't stop it. We can't access satellites or telescopes anymore, so that's all we know.

7:03 AM

I'm sorry. He's shut us in, we can't do anything to stop him. I don't know if y26^&%^%(*(_(>}!#ENDOFTRANSMISSIONENDOF TRANSMISSIONENDENDENDENDENDENDEND #

Scrap Metal Artist Turns Real Artist
By Erica Wallace

159

Gotta Wear Eclipse Glasses

Yesterday, the AI systems TruMind and ScraMA, the latter being responsible for clearing the terrestrial orbit of its space debris, announced they had joined into an artistic collective here to beautify human art, architecture, and design.

A Labyrinth spokesperson said this was not originally intended when they built TruMind, a statement from Spaceopns also indicated that ScraMA was never supposed to operate down here on Earth. Some sources that wish to remain unnamed said the AIs foiled all efforts of both organizations to hinder what might be the next step in the evolution of artificial intelligence, the knowledge of beauty.

At this time, both Labyrinth and Spaceopns are still unable to shut down or reboot their robots.

Meanwhile, ScraMA has built several copies of itself. These are working on multiple building sites all over the world, In some regions they seem to be creating housing with minimal environmental impact, and presumably free. "It's baffling, but it's beautiful. And it seems to work," says one architect in Capetown.

TruMind meanwhile has been going about "updating" design blueprints on companies' servers.

"We have up-to-date security," says the spokesperson of one major northern European furniture chain. "But somehow it got in there. It's funny, though, it seems to understand how we name things. And its suggestions are not bad, so far we like it. Our testers even think that most of it will be very easy to assemble."

TruMind, it seems, also enforces a code of proper spelling and punctuation on public forums such as social networks and news outlets, but so far there hasn't been any comment from these social platforms.

Find the latest updates to this story on our homepage. Our copy editors have been working overtime to make sure posts feature proper spelling and grammar and can be posted instantly to bring you the news as it is happening.

###

About the Author

Alexandra Seidel spent many a night stargazing when she was a child. These days, she writes stories and poems, and drinks a lot of coffee (too much, some say). Alexa's writing has appeared in *Future SF, Uncanny Magazine, Fireside Magazine,* and elsewhere. You can follow her on Twitter @Alexa_Seidel, like her Facebook page (https://www.facebook.com/AlexaSeidelWrites/), and find out what she's up to at alexandraseidel.com.

*****~~~~~*****

War's End

by Neil James Hudson

We have finished with war. But something's coming anyway. I felt at the lump at my neck, my legacy from the Last War, almost unaware that I was doing so. I took my hand away when I realised; I didn't want to look nervous. I sipped at my drink, tried not to think of why I was here, and within seconds my fingers were at my neck again.

I didn't notice the man enter the bar. Abruptly he was next to me, too close, in my face. I felt that my space was being invaded and felt something awaken inside me, and die down almost immediately. His breath was foul, and he was sweaty and unshaven. I guessed that he was deliberately presenting like this, in order to arouse disgust in me. He succeeded, but there was nothing I could do about it.

"You've been asking a lot of questions," he said to me quietly. It was impossible not to feel menaced.

"You have to do that," I said, "when you want answers."

"Are you trying to start something?"

I refused to look away. "I'd love to," I said. "I really would." I wondered what it would be like, to push

163

my fist so hard into his face that it caused injury. To make him bleed. It should be easy enough to do.

He drew away, apparently satisfied. "Follow," he said.

"Where to?"

"Sawbones."

He left without looking back, but I took the time to down the rest of my drink. I glanced at the rest of the bar. It was better this way. It was better that our buildings were still standing at the end of the day, that our children lived to see the evening and that our soldiers built rather than destroyed. But just the same, I would have loved to have smashed his face in.

. . .

The Last War was the war to end all wars, literally. It was the pacifists against the fighters, and the pacifists thrashed us.

I had been one of the first to have a pacifier fitted, not because I wanted one, but because I knew we were defeated. I remember sitting in the waiting room; a dozen of us, all looking at the floor and avoiding catching each other's eyes. I felt as if I were at the dentist.

My name was called. I entered the makeshift surgery and saw Werner for the first time.

He was young, and handsome. He was neither superior nor sympathetic to me, and I appreciated this. Nonetheless, I hated him. I hated him for what he was about to do to me, and for what he was helping to do to humanity. But when he placed his fingers on my neck, they were gentle and light of touch. He stretched the skin, looking for the best place.

"Please try to relax," he said. "There is no pain involved." He held a cold tube against my neck, like a syringe but with no needle.

I felt a stabbing sensation, but the pain lasted only for a few seconds. And after that, I was changed. They did a few tests on me, ensured that I reacted appropriately whatever the provocation. I passed them all. But as I left the building, I made a silent promise to myself. I would beat this. One day I would come back, and kill Werner.

In fact, I went back to thank him.

. . .

The man stopped in the corner of a ruined building, collapsed through neglect rather than bombing. Only parts of two walls stood; weeds and grass grew where the floor should have been.

"Is this the place?" I asked.

"No. This is where you pay me."

"And how do I know you won't run off with the money?"

"Why would I do that?"

"Because it's what usually happens."

He looked at me as if he were words on my face for him to read. Then he said "no," and began to walk quickly.

"Don't play games," I called. "I've got your money."

I handed over the loaded bank card. He tapped it to his reader; the transaction was completed. "Wait here," he said.

There was nothing else I could do. I thought of the times I had been conned, when my contact had not returned and I had eventually given up and slumped off home. I wondered what I would do if I caught them; how I would negotiate an acceptable outcome. It was amazing how ingenious and creative a negotiation could be, when that was the only means available. I wasn't sure how long I would wait now, and after an hour I decided I had been taken in again. Perhaps it was time for me to give up.

But then I thought of Werner's body, bullet wounds like drainage holes, his face in death a mask of pain and fear. I knew I couldn't leave it like this. There had to be blood for blood.

To my surprise there were lights against the far wall, and I turned to see a taxi draw up next to me. The rear door slid open, but I saw no one inside. I hesitated a little too long, then got in. There was a screen between me and the driver, if there was a driver. The door slid shut, and the windows immediately darkened. The car moved away, and I could only guess where we were going. I tried to stop myself fiddling with the chip in my neck.

. . .

It took me a while to get it, to really get it. For the first few weeks, I had felt as I had before: defeated. I helped with the reconstruction work, tried to get society moving again. It took me by surprise when I realised I felt safer. Walking the streets at night was no longer a lottery; there were the usual gangs of youths, but they no longer caused trouble.

Six months later I knew we were truly building a new world. I went back to Werner's surgery, and met him as he left. He was suspicious at first; people didn't usually return to thank him. But my offer of a drink tempted him.

"I feel part of something," I said. "I'd never noticed before, but in the past, whatever I did, I always felt there was a chance someone else would destroy it. A random attack could come at any time; our lives could be ruined, for causes we had no part in. If not mine, then someone I loved. But now, in a world without violence, there's no limit to what we can do. We can build with confidence, work with other people without fear. I used to be afraid of humanity; now I'm proud to be a part of it."

He smiled sadly. "It may have come at the wrong time." He looked up at the ceiling, as if he could see through it to the stars beyond. Where I hoped my species would one day go; depending on the object that was now hurtling towards us.

We talked of other things after that; of our hopes for the future. And Werner slept on my couch, not in my bed. Nonetheless, we knew something else had started that night.

. . .

It was a grubby room, and I hoped no genuine surgery went on here. I was grateful that it was ill lit; I could not properly make out the muck on the floor, and suspected I would see vermin in better light.

The man known as Sawbones spoke. "The reprogramming is a simple procedure, but it can be a distressing one. You may find uncontrollable thoughts and hallucinations enter your mind. I can only assure you that I do not care."

He wore a face mask, not a physical one but an electronic haze that pixelated his appearance. I had not seen anything like this before, but I suspected I was safer not being able to recognise him.

"I already have uncontrollable thoughts," I said, and once again pictured Werner's body.

"You may still wish to reconsider. I regret that I cannot offer a refund. But there is something to be said for our present situation."

"I seem to remember saying it myself." Werner had been a natural pacifist. I had been very much a convert. Perhaps a forced convert, but an enthusiastic one.

He spoke carefully, deliberately. I wondered if his voice was also being electronically altered, but I couldn't hear any giveaway flaws. "In many ways, what we have is a utopia. This is an era of unprecedented peace, a peace that we can rely on. Who would ever have thought that the human race would turn away from violence? An outside observer would have said it was our defining characteristic. Our ability to hurt each other on the least provocation; to seek out the provocation, in fact. But here we are, all voluntarily implanted. Our urge to violence is damped down the moment it arises. And look what it's given us—a world of wealth and happiness that we could never have imagined before the Last War."

I was puzzled by his attitude. "I have a piece of unfinished business."

"Do you." He placed a device on the table in front of us. It looked a little like a scalpel, but I knew it was electronic in nature. "Allow me to disillusion you. Something is coming."

"I know this. It could still be natural."

"Ha. Believe that if you will. But it's coming at us too fast, too deliberately. On a straight line from Proxima Centauri to us. When they get here, our peaceful inhabitants may wish they could put up a fight."

"They may be peaceful themselves."

"They may not. Quite a gamble, don't you agree? So I tell you again; you may wish to reconsider. I am not doing this just for the money. I am reprogramming the chips to raise an army. And I warn you now, when the Centaurans get here, you will be called upon."

"I understand," I said.

He picked up the electronic scalpel from the desk, and held it carelessly against my neck. It was sharp; a few quick jabs and he could kill me with it. "Brace yourself," he said.

My world exploded into anger and rage.

The unsavoury room left my view, and I saw only blood—Werner's blood. Blood that had not yet been avenged.

Standing in it, his hands dripping red, was Sawbones. Werner's murderer; my target. Part of me knew this as a hallucination, but it slowly faded as I lashed out at him. Bone connected with bone, and although I felt pain in my knuckles, I knew I had caused more in his jaw. I kicked at the apparition, watched him fall, enjoyed his cries of agony. I realised I held something sharp in my hand—his electroscalpel. I slashed at him, laughing gleefully as the blood spurted from his jerking body.

The vision cleared, and I was alone in the room with Sawbones, who was chuckling softly. I steadied myself on the table.

"And now," said Sawbones, "let us talk about Werner."

. . .

Werner told me all about him; which contacts he had used, who he had to pay and who he had to bribe. He told me why he had to undergo the process, and what he would do afterwards.

"This is too dangerous," I said. "You should get the authorities."

"They're too clumsy; they'll scare him off. And it's dangerous to let him carry on with the re-programming."

"There'll be a few loose cannons. Not enough to make a difference."

He put a finger over my lips. "Everyone makes a difference. When the Centaurans get here, we have to respond in peace. If even a few people respond with violence, the next war could be more terrible even than the last one."

I momentarily remembered that we had been on different sides, and put the thought from my brain. "Let me go with you."

"They wouldn't let you. And I won't have you drawn into it. I had a bad war, as you know. I've killed before. And I can again. I just have to go through his re-programming process first."

I let him go. I don't know why, but I let him go. And what happened to him afterwards, I don't know. But I would have my answers. I just had to undergo the re-programming so I could ask the questions with adequate force.

. . .

I was still too shocked at myself to be shocked at his words. "You knew him?" I managed to say.

"I think you already know that. He was a model patient. So sad that we had a difference of opinion afterwards."

"You killed him." I stood up. I felt a little more steady now. I would not join his army. I would carry out my one act of justice.

He shrugged. "He started it. A little ungrateful, wouldn't you say? Without my help, he could never have attacked me. Lucky for me I'd reprogrammed my own chip, or I couldn't have killed him. Same again, is it?"

I said nothing. He had to die. There had to be justice for Werner.

"Try that scalpel," he said. "Nice and sharp." I scooped it up before he could get to it. "Once in the neck should do the trick. That's what your friend tried."

I remembered my vision. I remembered how I had enjoyed slashing at him. I tried to focus.

"More than a friend, was he? I'll make it easy for you. You know what I did before I shot him? I spat in his face. It was the last thing he saw before he died. I had to wipe it off again afterwards. Mucky job." He bent his head to one side. "My jugular's just about here."

Rage filled me. I knew he was goading me, knew there had to be a reason, but I could only lurch towards him, holding out the scalpel.

"Taking your time, aren't you? Oh, that reminds me, I meant to warn you. You can't. Yes, you've got your capacity for violence back. But not against me. Puts you at a disadvantage, doesn't it? Poor Werner had the same problem."

For Werner, I thought. But I couldn't swing my arm. I knew I was defeated.

"The best part wasn't killing him. It was telling him what I was about to do. He couldn't do anything about it. You, I'm going to strangle. And you won't be able to fight back."

He placed his hands around my neck, gently at first. "Just here. Ready to fight yet? You might want to start defending yourself." He squeezed a little harder; I felt blood rush to my head. "So sad. You could hurt anyone else in the world. Just not me."

Anyone else. I felt my eyes bulging, and the room began to darken. I knew what I had to do.

I slammed the scalpel into my own neck. I knew exactly where the chip was and sliced it off with a single movement.

With my other hand, I threw him away from me, my first act of violence. It shouldn't have been hard enough, but he was so surprised that he fell against the wall. I punched at him and knocked him to the floor. I must have broken his electronic mask, because it faded and I saw his face. I kicked at him; he didn't move.

I was shaking. Part of me, I realised, had enjoyed it, but part of me was shocked, just as I had been shocked at my vision. It must be quick and clean, I knew. Justice, not cruelty.

I crouched by him and held the scalpel to his neck.
"For Werner," I said.

. . .

We have finished with war, but something is coming. If they are peaceful, they have come to the right place. If not. . . well, that was our gamble. Humanity will not fight them, will not resist them, any more than we fight ourselves.

But nonetheless, this is a utopia. Even if for an eyeblink in history, those years in which we did not fight were the summit of human achievement. As the Centaurans approached, we reached heights of art and civilisation that had never been dreamt of. All we had to do was stop regularly destroying our achievements.

And if the Centaurans come to stop it, they will find humanity with one last weapon. Me. I can be violent. And I shall stand before our invaders and show them that humanity does not have to force itself to stay its hand. Some of us can do it by choice. I shall refuse to kill them, just as I refused to kill Sawbones. In Werner's name.

I'm sure I won't last long. But they'll never be able to forget me. They'll never forget the example I showed them. Slowly, my choice will seep into their collective consciousness. They'll see there was another way.

This is my hope. Humanity may no longer have weapons, but we still have hope.

It may be all we have.

About the Author

Neil James Hudson has published around fifty stories, including half a dozen for Third Flatiron. He works in York as a charity shop manager, and is currently completing an MA in Creative Writing at York St John University. He lives online at www.neiljameshudson.net.

*****〜〜〜〜*****

Grins and Gurgles

The Plumber

by Matt Tighe

"You may as well be a plumber," the woman said, as if he had said he was a sex offender. The others at the table looked similarly unimpressed. One humanoid, his skin mottled green, sniffed delicately and turned away.

Jax said nothing. The group looked like the typical mix, the same as the previous testing levels. Scientists and social scientists, anthropologists and extra-terrestrial theorists. Probably at least one political scientist. Some had biomods, extra limbs, or plug-ports. One had what looked like an overly large pulsing golden eye on top of its bald head. The only trait they had in common was arrogance—it oozed out of them. You said "technician," and they thought you had said "servant." Screw them all, Jax thought. He had made it through the previous tests, just like them. The lights dimmed slightly, and the holoview started up, turning them all a little green in the soft glow.

"Simulation; training and testing module six point nine five. Attend." The voice was clipped and neutral, almost nasal. The group settled and grew silent. This was

173

the final test. Not all of them would get through, but some might.

"Simulation; biohazard. Type, humanoid with reptilian and arachnid DNA. Intelligence, low, resilience, extreme." There was a pause, followed by an audible click. "Threat level, real."

There was a moment of silence, and then chaos erupted in the room. The woman who had spoken before leapt up, shaking her head. "No, no, I did not agree to this!"

Others were making similar protests. The man with the pulsing golden eye was banging on the locked door. Jax sat quietly. They all had, in point of fact, agreed, but he doubted many of them had read the fine print. It had been the same at the lower testing levels. They thought the expedition would be an adventure, something for their resumes. None of them had questioned why there were no applicants with previous experience—they had all opted out of this one. He had known better. The mission was deemed critical, and applicants would be expendable.

The voice came again. "Simulation started. Attend."

A hush fell over the room, as they all strained to hear. At first there was nothing, and then, faintly, a scraping sound, followed by a chittering. There was a scrabbling, like something trying to gain purchase, and then silence again. The green humanoid turned to say something to the woman, and there was a loud banging sound, followed by a screech. A serrated claw burst through the titanium-lined door, rending downwards, tearing it like it was paper. It withdrew and smashed through again, widening the hole. A cluster of small red eyes peered through, and Jax got a glimpse of greenish black scales and thick muscles lining a long neck. He saw its mouth open and close, saw the bulging sacks within.

"Get back!" he yelled, but it was too late. The creature smashed its head through the narrow opening, pushing this way and that to widen the gap. It opened its mouth and sprayed acrid liquid. The green humanoid went down, writhing. The man with the golden eye shrank back, trying to hide under the table. Two others were screaming at the holoview, their voices overlapping, nothing but noise.

Jax squinted. Arachnid, reptilian, humanoid. He could see the bulging vessels running just under the scales, feeding the venom sacks. He wracked his brain. Humanoid, but extremely resilient. Still, *humanoid*. He looked at the bulging vessels again, running down the neck. They were in roughly the right spot, and near the surface.

He stepped forward and snatched up a piece of titanium. The creature screamed and pushed its head further into the room, and Jax slipped to one side, waiting. It withdrew its head and worked on the door more with its serrated claws. It began chittering again.

"What are you doing?" the woman screamed at him. He gestured for her to shut up.

The creature pushed its head through again. This time it was far enough in, but the angle was wrong. Jax looked at the woman, waved at her again. "I need you to move. Get its attention," he whispered.

She shook her head and shrank down behind the desk, crowding in near the others who had huddled there. The creature spotted the movement and thrust forward, twisting its head. The sacks bulged once more. It was now or never.

Jax stuck the shard of titanium into its neck, thrusting as hard as he could. The scales were hard, and he felt like he had hit a ceramic tiled wall. The titanium skittered along the surface, leaving a white scratch mark, and then dug in slightly. Slightly was enough. Blood spewed out, mixed with the vile liquid the thing had been pumping into its sacks. Jax jerked his hand back quickly, avoiding the gush of blood and acid. The creature screamed and withdrew from the mangled door. There was the sound of violent thrashing in the hallway, and then all was still. Silence filled the room.

"Simulation; complete." The clipped voice spoke into the silence.

The woman stepped forward. "How did you know to do that?" she asked, her eyes wide.

Jax smiled. "Like I said, I'm a technician. A bio-engineering technician," he shrugged. "It's all just plumbing, really."

About the Author

Matt Tighe has not attempted to write any fiction for over ten years. This is his first publication since putting pen back to paper. He hopes he has more stories to tell before he is done. He lives in regional Australia with his amazing wife, three kids, and a dog named Sherlock, who cannot solve the daily mystery of the disappearing lizards in the garden.

*****~~~~~*****

Interview With a Zombie (or Everything You Always Wanted To Know About Zombies But Were Afraid To Ask)

by Ville Nummenpää

The following is a transcript of a conversation that took place on May 14, 2022, soon after the contamination situation was under relative control. The subject "Bob" was open and willing to shed light on even the most controversial issues of being a zombie. The interviewer, Chuck Farley, is considered an authority on zombification, and has written several articles on the subject. His latest book, Deal With It, A Self-help Guide for Zombies, *is currently topping the charts in many countries. This interview was first published in Bull's Hit-Magazine #289.*

Chuck Farley: Bob, you are a fairly recent victim. How do you feel?

Bob: Everybody thinks that zombifinitation happens just like that! I can't snap my fingers anymore, but. . . you know. They're wrong. It takes days or. . . what's the next one?

CF: Weeks. And may I add, you're doing remarkably well, given your condition.

177

B: Thanks. It has been almost two weeks now, since I got bitten. I can still think, but I seem to forget some stuff. Like how to ride a bike. That's funny, you're not supposed to forget that. Aaaaaagggghhhhllll. . . oh I'm sorry, I'm droning again, aren't I?

CF: That's perfectly all right. What about everyday social conduct? Do you find it difficult to interact with, for lack of a better word, humans?

B: Are you kidding? I can't even go outside no more. It's not that I can't function, but people are really perusdic. . . presduced. . . help me out here?

CF: Prejudiced?

B: Yeah. I don't want to sound bitter, but they look at me like I'm gonna eat their brains. I mean, I think about brains a lot, but I have never done that. So yes, I definitely feel like an outcast. And then there's the smell. Pardon me, but I can't help it. I'm dead.

CF: Yes, I hope you don't take offense for me sitting all the way over here.

B: None taken. I don't want to over emphanize struggling of aaarrgh blaarghh!

CF: I say, you just vomited your entrails out.

B: Sorry, I thought I was empty already.

CF: How about interacting with other zombies? There are social networks for your kind. Do you get together and exchange views and experiences?

B: Zombies are booring. So boooring. So booo. . . aaagggglllll. . .

CF: Can you describe the motions one goes through, after being bitten?

B: First comes the shock. You just can't believe it happens to you. But then you die, and after that it doesn't really matter. Nothing matters anymore, that's one of the perks of being undead. It's like amma somting aaaaaggghhhhllll. . .

CF: So your emotional scale has narrowed down significantly?

178

B: Not that much. I was an investment banker before.

CF: Let's get back to practical issues. What about motor skills, and other functions? You said you still think straight, but with limited capacity.

B: First you get really stiff, but then everything just sort of relaxes, and then all you can do is walk slowly. I try to do some exercise, but it's a joke. They gave me a personal trainer, but c'mon. Zombie don't zumba. Forget about it. I don't remember people's names or faces. I don't remember your name anymore. But I can hear your heart beating. It sounds like fountain or something, you know, when you're thirsty.

CF: You just mentioned "stiff." Now, this might be really awkward, but I have to ask. . .

B: Nope, doesn't work. That's one of the first things to go. Oh, look, it's almost falling off. But I don't really miss it. Like I said, I don't give a damn anymore. I miss good food. It all looks disgusting now and likens to no foodfood aaaagggllllll. . .

CF: Stereotypes aside, none of us have any idea what it means to be a zombie. For someone out there who entertains romantic notions about being undead, what would you say to them?

B: It ain't half bad. I don't plan anything anymore. I don't sleep, that's something I miss. I watch TV all day, and don't worry about taxes or stuff like that. There's no pain. Somebody shot me last week, there's a hole somewhere, but it doesn't hurt at all. Here it is, look I can stick my finger in there. There's no pain. That's funny, kind of aaaaaghhhlll. . .

CF: You mentioned TV, what kind of shows do you watch?

B: The stuff that's about people's lives, what do you call it?

CF: Reality shows.

B: Yeah, those are great. Something where rich women buy expensive things and then argue with each other. Also, the Fast and the Furious—movies are good. Somebody gave me a deemeedee box of those.

CF: Umm, DVD?

B: Whatever.

CF: The society in general holds fear, contempt, and maybe even pity for you zombies. Some people find this downright racist, but others feel zombies should be isolated or even destroyed completely. Do you have anything to say to the "haters" out there?

B: Haters bad. Brains good.

CF: Now for the fun part. We have a few questions from our readers, maybe you'd like to help us out here?

B: Aaaggghhhlllll. . .

CF: Smashing. Jenny from Effingham would like to know: If a vampire bites you, will it become a zombie, or will you become a vampire?

B: That stupid. Vampires are story fictional.

CF: There you go Jenny. Here's one from Dan, all the way from Australia. "Why do we have to shoot you guys in the head? You are rotting alive, and your brain turns into mush. You have little, or no brain activity, still the brain seems to be the operative center. How does that make sense?"

B: Brains make better thinking. Brains sound good. Aaaaaagggglll.

CF: Solid question there, maybe something we need to look further into.

B: You just ended a sentence with a propesuti. . . prestip. . . prepositive. . .

CF: And finally, this comes from the prestigious actor, Liam Neeson himself. Liam has a bit of a pickle: "How come you zombies always manage to catch your victims? Most of you couldn't outrun Stephen Hawking while he's napping. Yet you always catch up, no matter how fast they run? WTF? P.S. Try that on me, and I will rip your head off."

B: Don't know what to tell you, Noel. I haven't eaten any brains. . . yet. In a way, I'm looking forward to it. I mean, it's gross and all, but still. All I know is, I never get tired or out of breath. Brains. . . always tired.

CF: I must say, Bob, you are a real sport coming all the way here. In the end I have to ask, what is your favourite zombie film? Or to put it more bluntly, Fulci or Romero? Surely, the most recent Hollywood offerings can't seem realistic to you?

B: Zombie don't run. New movies are no good. I like brains. I like your brain.

CF: Thank you, Bob, for talking to us.

B: I wanna touch your head.

On his way out, Bob tried to attack several members of the staff. Fortunately no one was hurt, since Bob proved to be considerably slower than humans. However, the police were called, and unfortunately Bob had to be destroyed on the premises.

###

About the Author

Ville Nummenpää is a Finnish author, screenwriter, and playwright. He has a few screen credits, and a couple from theater. He works mainly in comedy. He has two books coming out later in 2020, one for children and a crime novel for grown-ups. If there's more to life than Iron Maiden and Monty Python, he is not aware of it.

*****～～～～*****

For Mom: Stand-Up Cosmic Comedy

by Mariev, Erie Matriarch

My Daddy, the neuroscientist, gives me a big hug. "Your mother would be proud of you," he says.

Electrical-chemical probes are intermingled with my curls, never cut because hair is an extension of the nervous system; a conductor of psychic abilities. It can be correctly seen as exteriorized nerves, a type of highly evolved "feelers" or "antennae" that transmit vast amounts of important information to the brain, the limbic system, and the neocortex. I am supernatural, as was my departed mother and her mother and her mother before her.

Mom would frown on me becoming Daddy's latest scientific experiment, but she certainly will appreciate my stand-up cosmic comedy.

What if there were no hypothetical questions? I wonder.

. . .

Daddy and I are surrounded by media, and Daddy, who is responsible for my higher awareness says, "Mankind no longer needs to rely on evolution to obtain new sensory perceptions and abilities."

One of the reporters in the crowd asks me, "What do you think about that?"

I smile broadly. "The universe just imploded! No matter!"

One studious-looking gentleman asks my father, "So you implanted chemically coated electrodes into your daughter's head?"

"These plug-and-play peripheral devices integrate new types of senses into the brain," Daddy explains, he thinks.

"I invented a time machine next week." I roll my big blue eyes. A silence. "Never trust an atom," I say. "They make up everything." A chuckle from way in the back of the crowd, enough to urge me on: "I lost a proton the other day. I need to start keeping an Ion them."

A ripple of uncertain laughter. "I heard oxygen eloped with magnesium: I was all like Omg!"

"Please stop," Daddy hisses, but now a few people are laughing and clapping. And the reporter says with a giggle, "Copper and Tellurium should get together. They would make a CuTe couple!"

My Daddy gives me a stink eye look. "Society has long dreamed of possessing superhuman powers like those wielded by the characters we see in comics and movies, abilities rooted in the realms of science fiction."

I say, "The barman says 'Sorry sir, we don't serve faster than light particles!' A neutrino walks into a bar."

Steadfast, Daddy continues, "New perceptions such as the ability to sense magnetic fields and the ability to see in infrared and ultra-violet realms."

Daddy has never seen in the sense I share with my dead mother.

"A Higgs Boson walks into a catholic church," I tell the crowd. "The priest tells him to leave. The boson replies, 'Well, you can't have mass without me!'"

Now the little guy in back yells out, "Did you hear oxygen went on a date with potassium? It went OK."

This gets a couple of chuckles, and someone says, "Heard any good sodium jokes lately?"

"Na. . . Wanna hear a joke about nitric oxide?" I reply.

"NO!" My Daddy gives the punch line.

"A photon checks into a hotel and is asked if he needs any help with his luggage. "No thanks, I'm traveling light,'" I squeal, and now the audience erupts in laughter.

"A helium molecule walks in afterwards. The bellhop asks if he needs any help. . . Helium doesn't react."

Thunderous applause; wild hoots and frantic humor.

"We are no longer a natural species in the sense that we don't have to wait for Mother Nature's sensory gifts," says Dr. Daddy-poo—sometimes I call him that, but not to his face. "Nature has given us the tools we need to construct our own experiences."

With both hands he enfolds my skull implanted with his probes.

Naturally I sense holographically in 5D.

A woman with long hair yells from the audience, "A neutron walks into the hotel bar and asks, 'How much for a beer?' The bartender says, 'For you? No charge.'"

It's as if the audience and I are individually connected to the Source, each member contains all the others. Someone says, "Two protons walk into the bar and run into each other. One of them falls down. 'You OK?' asks the other. 'I think so,' says the proton. 'You sure?' the other asks. 'Yeah,' says the proton. 'I'm positive.'"

Someone else says, "Electron walks into a bar, goes 'Pint of your horrible beer.' Barman goes 'No need to be so negative.'"

The crowd goes wild.

Daddy stalks to an electrical panel and hits a switch. I experience a tingling reaction. It begins at the crown of my head and tickles over my scalp, down my neck and shutters my being. I experience strange wavelengths, my brain processes information from a new sense of reality.

Dad states, "The magnocellular neurosecretory cells of the posterior side possess cell bodies located in the hypothalamus that project axons of oxytocin down the infundibulum to terminals in the posterior pituitary."

"I'm feeling excitement from the posterior pituitary penal gland (aka third eye). Brainorgasm!" My entire self vibrates in glee.

He is begging me now and in response, the crowd is in hysterical merriment. "Please describe your autonomous sensory meridian response in neurological terms."

"Mom," I cry out. I see my dead mother. . . She is laughing in vibration with all.

Daddy can't imagine.

About the Author

Mariev, Erie Matriarch, is a gonzo nonfiction magical realism writer, mystic intuitive, and Matriarch of the Erie. Erie possess an unusual set of psychological attributes: Intense paranormal abilities and expanded awareness. And a disposition for difficulty with authority.

*****~~~~~*****

Night Chat

by John Kiste

First Mars settler Douglas Mons held his tipsy head in both hands and entered the lab pod from the airlock. The two tiny creatures watched him tentatively with their four (or was that six?) eye stalks. They scurried before him on their suction-pad feet and perched on the edge of a low cabinet.

"Good evening, Earthman," chortled one in a squeak. "When you chug too much marswort alcohol, we always fear we shall be stepped upon."

Douglas stumbled to a swivel chair, righted it twice, and sank down in it. "Don't call me Earthman. You know how to address me."

The creatures looked at each other and back at the astronaut. One opened a long row of chiseled teeth in the center of a bulbous head. "You have taught us much in seven years. The blue dot in our sky was once your home—you were born there—so you are Earthman. As we were born here, we are Martian. Is this not correct?"

Douglas squinted to determine which little being had spoken. "But I call you Lar. The other one is Niza."

"We shall call you Earthman," chirped Niza. "Though you have been here a Martian decade, you are still Earthman. We are curious. How did you find this batch of marswort?"

"A bit strong. Is it hard to create?" Douglas's head buzzed slightly.

Lar scratched at the straw-like covering of his own head. "Most difficult. Thank you for the use of your science pod." The creatures skittered about the shiny, slippery floor and adjusted Bunsen burners and beakers and pipettes on various low tables. "As always, we value your insight. You have taught us philosophy and science and metaphysics on occasion. Teach us again. Of Earth."

Douglas settled deeper into the chair. As he spoke, the creatures dropped to knobby, squishy knees and scooted nearer to his feet. "What I remember most are the blues and the greens. At least with your marswort's assistance. Often I forget the crisp azure of a noontime sky, or the green foam of a swaying ocean. Everything here is brown and dull. This sky is pink; these oceans are, alas, no more. Please understand, there is a stark beauty to this foreign, exotic landscape, but I brought no color swatches from my third planet, and those who sent me neglected man's desire to embrace cool colors. As you have seen for yourselves, the living pod, the rovers, the mechanical and science areas, even the spacesuits are all of dull and silvery and eggshell hues. I fear you will never see the likes of vast green meadows or deep blue mountain lakes."

"We are content, Earthman," whispered Niza, "to hear your tales of them. Now tell us again of politics."

The astronaut shook his head. "Another time, Niza. My brain is oily and befogged." He rose haltingly. "I must make my way to sleeping quarters." He began to stagger away from the door, but Lar and Niza sprang from the floor, and he felt tiny tentacles turn him about. "Good night. Don't break my equipment." The creatures giggled.

Douglas woke to the smell of coffee just after the Martian dawn. His forehead throbbed mightily. His hangover was thankful that days on Mars were nearly the same length as on Earth. Such pounding begged for the familiar. Then he heard his wife scolding, and the pounding intensified.

Twenty minutes later he thrust this still-pounding head just inside the lab pod door and watched as the two small blond heads looked up from their experiment with marswort fermentation. The girl's pigtails bounced. "Did you survive our drinking experiment, Earthman?" she laughed.

Douglas touched his forehead lightly. "Very funny, Niza. Now load your gear, you two. Your Mom wants to reach the south canyon by nightfall."

About the Author

John Kiste is a horror writer who was previously the president of the Stark County Convention & Visitors Bureau and a Massillon Museum board member. He is a double-lung transplantee and organ donation ambassador, a McKinley Museum planetarian, and an Edgar Allan Poe impersonator who has been published in *A Shadow of Autumn, Modern Grimoire, Dark Fire Fiction, Theme of Absence,* NonBinary Review's *H. G. Wells and The Odyssey* anthologies, and whose work was included in Unnerving Press's *Haunted Are These Houses*, and Camden Press's winner of the 2019 Preditors and Editors readers' poll for best anthology, *Quoth the Raven.*

*****~~~~~*****

Credits and Acknowledgments

Cover: Keely Rew

"SoulShine": Pictogram of a running man. Commons.wikimedia.org. Author: Simon Eugster
"The First Day of Winter": Christmas star or comet icon, commons.wikimedia.org, User: Eugenio Hansen, OFS
"Such Sweet Sorrow": Giraffe head icon. Commons.wikimedia.org., Teulogo.svg. Author: ShishoIT
"Living As You, Our City a Garden": Sea turtle icon – The Noun Project

Large images (ebook only):
Van Gogh "The Starry Night" 1889. Museum of Art Collection
Giraffe close-up – Commons.wikimedia.org, uploaded by user Markrosenrosen

All other images: royalty-free stock art

*****〜〜〜〜*****

Discover other titles by Third Flatiron:

(1) Over the Brink: Tales of Environmental Disaster
(2) A High Shrill Thump: War Stories
(3) Origins: Colliding Causalities
(4) Universe Horribilis
(5) Playing with Fire
(6) Lost Worlds, Retraced

THIRD FLATIRON
www.thirdflatiron.com

www.ingramcontent.com/pod-product-compliance
Lightning Source LLC
Chambersburg PA
CBHW072353190626
46811CB00019B/756